"You're a lawyer, huh?" asked the small-town police chief.

"Well, Counselor, whose battle are you here to win?"

Anne's mouth tightened. But then, one hardly expected the police to look kindly on defense attorneys. And most times the feeling was mutual.

"I'm representing myself." She glanced down at eight-month-old Emilie, who banged her rattle on the stroller tray. "And my daughter. I'm here because..." How could she say this?

She forced the words out. "Because I believe you are Emilie's biological father."

Chief Mitch Donovan stared at her, shifted the stare to the baby, then back to her. If his eyes had softened slightly before, when they assessed Emilie, that softness turned to granite now when his gaze met hers.

"Lady, you're crazy. I've never seen you before in my life."

D0815992

Books by Marta Perry

Love Inspired

A Father's Promise #41
Since You've Been Gone #75
Desperately Seeking Dad #91

*Hometown Heroes

MARTA PERRY

wanted to be a writer from the moment she encountered Nancy Drew, at about age eight. She didn't see publication of her stories until many years later, when she began writing children's fiction for Sunday school papers while she was a church education director. Although now retired from that position in order to write full-time, she continues to play an active part in her church and loves teaching a class of lively fifth- and sixth-grade Sunday school students.

The author lives in rural Pennsylvania with her husband of thirty-seven years. They have three grown children.

Desperately Seeking Dad
Marta Perry

Love Inspired®

Published by Steeple Hill Books™

STEEPLE HILL BOOKS

Steeple
Hill™

ISBN 0-373-87097-3

DESPERATELY SEEKING DAD

Printed in U.S.A.

Trust in the Lord with all your heart and lean not on your own understanding; in all your ways acknowledge Him, and He will direct your paths.

—*Proverbs* 3:5-6

In loving memory of my parents-in-law, Harry and Greta Johnson. And, as always, for Brian.

Chapter One

"**I** believe you're my baby's father." Anne Morden tried saying it aloud as she drove down the winding street of the small mountain town. The words sounded just as bad as she'd thought they would. There was absolutely no good way to announce a fact like that to a man she'd never met.

In her mind and heart, Emilie was already her child, even though the adoption wasn't yet final—even though the father hadn't yet relinquished his rights.

He would. Fear closed around her heart. He had to. Because if he didn't, she might lose the baby she loved as her own.

The soft sound of a rattle drew her gaze to the rearview mirror. Emilie, safe in her car seat, shook the pink plastic lamb with one chubby fist, then stuck it in her mouth. At eight months, Emilie put everything in her mouth.

"It'll be all right, sweetheart. I promise."

Emilie's round blue eyes got a little rounder, and her face crinkled into a smile at the sound of Anne's voice...the voice of the only mother the baby had ever known.

Fear prickled along her nerves. She had to protect Emilie, had to make sure the adoption went through as planned so the baby would truly be hers. And confronting the man she believed to be Emilie's biological father was the only way to do that. But where were the right words?

Anne spotted the faded red brick building ahead on the right, its black-and-white sign identifying it as the police station. Her heart clenched. She'd face Police Chief Mitch Donovan in a matter of minutes, and she still didn't know what she'd say.

Help me, Father. Please. For Emilie's sake, let me find a way to do this.

A parking spot waited for her in front of the station. She couldn't drive around for a few more minutes. Now, before she lost her nerve, she had to go inside, confront the man, and get his signature on a parental rights termination.

For Emilie. Emilie was her child, and nobody, including the unknown Mitch Donovan, was going to take her away.

Parking the car, getting the stroller out, buttoning Emilie's jacket against the cool, sunny March day—

none of that took long enough. With another silent, incoherent prayer, Anne pulled open the door and pushed the stroller inside.

Bedford Creek didn't boast much in the way of a police station—just a row of chairs, a crowded bulletin board and one desk. A small town like this, tucked safely away in the Pennsylvania mountains, probably didn't need more. She'd driven only three hours from Philadelphia, but Bedford Creek seemed light-years from the city, trapped in its isolated valley.

"Help you?" The woman behind the desk had dangling earrings that jangled as she spun toward Anne. Her penciled eyebrows shot upward, as if she were expecting an emergency.

"I'd like to see Chief Donovan, please." Her voice didn't betray her nervousness, at least she didn't think so.

That was one of the first things she'd learned as an attorney—never let her apprehension show, not if she wanted to win. And this was far more important than any case she'd ever defended.

The woman studied her for a moment, then nodded. "Chief!" she shouted. "Somebody to see you!"

Apparently the police station didn't rely on such high-tech devices as phones. The door to the inner office started to move. Anne braced herself. In a moment she'd—

The street door flew open, hitting the wall. An

elderly man surged in from outside, white hair standing on end as if he'd just run his fingers through it. He was breathing hard, and his face was an alarming shade of red. He propelled a dirty-faced boy into the room with a hand on the child's jacket collar.

The man emerging from the chief's office sent her a quick look, seemed to decide her business wasn't urgent, and focused on the pair who'd stormed in.

"Warren, what's going on?" His voice was a baritone rumble, filled with authority.

"This kid." The man shook the boy by his collar. "I caught him stealing from me again, Chief. Not one measly candy bar, no. He had a whole fist full of them."

Maybe she'd been wrong about the amount of crime in Bedford Creek. She was going to see Mitch Donovan in action before she even confronted him.

She looked at him, assessing the opposition as she would in a courtroom. Big, that was her first thought. The police uniform strained across broad shoulders. He had to be over six feet tall, with not an ounce of fat on him. If she'd expected the stereotypical small-town cop with his stomach hanging over his belt, she was wrong.

"So you decided to perform a citizen's arrest, did you, Warren?" The chief concentrated on the mismatched pair.

She couldn't tell whether or not amusement

lurked in his dark-brown eyes. He had the kind of strong, impassive face that didn't give much away.

"Not so old, after all, am I?" The elderly man gave his captive another little shake. "I caught you, all right."

"Take it easy." Donovan pulled the boy away. "You'll rattle the kid's brains."

The boy glared at the cop defiantly, eyes dark as two pieces of anthracite in his thin face, black hair that needed a trim falling on his forehead. He couldn't be more than ten or eleven, and he didn't appear to be easily intimidated. She wasn't sure she could have mustered a look like that—not with more than six feet of muscle looming over her.

"Okay, Davey, what's the story? You steal from Mr. Van Dyke?" His tone said there wasn't much doubt in his mind.

"Not me. Must have been somebody else."

The boy would have been better off to curb his smart remarks, but she'd defended enough juveniles to know he probably wouldn't.

"Empty your pockets," Donovan barked.

Davey held the defiant pose for another moment. Then he shrugged, reached into his jacket pockets and pulled them inside out. Five candy bars tumbled to the floor.

"You know what that is, kid? That's evidence."

"It's just a couple lousy candy bars."

"And I've got a couple lousy cells in the back. You want to see inside one of them?"

The kid wilted. "I don't…"

"Excuse me." Little as she wanted to become involved in this, she couldn't let it pass without saying something. Her training wouldn't let her. "The child's a minor. You shouldn't even be talking to him without a parent or legal representation here."

His piercing gaze focused on her, and she had to stiffen her spine to keep from wilting herself.

"That right, Counselor?"

He was quicker than she might have expected, realizing from those few words that she was an attorney.

"That's right." She glared at him, but the look seemed to have as much impact as a flake of snow on a boulder.

"If she says—" Davey caught on fast.

"Forget it." Donovan planted his forefinger against the boy's chest. "You're dealing with me, and if I hear another complaint against you, you'll wish you'd never been born. Stay out of Mr. Van Dyke's store until he tells you otherwise." He gestured toward the door. "Now get out."

The boy blinked. His first two steps were a swagger. Then he broke and ran, the door slamming behind him as he pelted up the sidewalk.

Anne took a breath and tried to force taut muscles to relax. At least now she didn't have to deal with Donovan over his treatment of the boy. Her own business with him was difficult enough.

The elderly man gathered the candy bars from the

floor, grumbling a little. "Kids. At least when you were his age, you only tried it once."

A muscle twitched in Donovan's jaw. Maybe he'd rather not have heard his juvenile crime mentioned, at least not with her standing there.

"You tripped me with a broom before I got to the door, as I recall. You slowing down, Warren?"

The old man shrugged. "Still give a kid a run for his money, I guess." He shoved the candy bars into his pockets. "I'm going to the café for a cup of coffee, now that I've done your work for you." He waved toward the dispatcher, then strolled out.

Donovan turned, studying her for a long, uncomfortable moment. Her cheeks warmed under his scrutiny. He gestured toward his office. "Come in, Counselor, and tell me what I can do for you."

This was it, then. She pushed the stroller through the door, heart thumping. This was it.

The swivel chair creaked as he sat down and waved her to the visitor's seat. Behind the battered oak desk, an American flag dwarfed the spare, small office. Some sort of military crest hung next to it. Donovan was ex-military, of course. Anne might have guessed it from his manner.

Maybe she should have remained standing. She always thought better on her feet, and she was going to need every edge she could get, dealing with this guy.

Anne leaned back, trying for a confidence she didn't feel, and resisted the urge to clench her hands.

Be calm, be poised. Check out the opposition, then act.

Mitch Donovan had that look she always thought of as the "cop look"—wary, tough, alert. Probably even in repose his stony face wouldn't relax. He could as easily be an Old West gunfighter, sitting with his back to the wall, ready to fly into action at the slightest provocation.

She took a deep breath. He was waiting for her to begin, but not the slightest movement of a muscle in his impassive face betrayed any hint of impatience. This was probably a man who'd buried his emotions so deep that a dynamite blast wouldn't make them surface.

"I realize I have no standing here, Chief Donovan, but you shouldn't have questioned the child without his parents." That wasn't what she'd intended to say, but it spilled out more easily than her real concern.

"I wasn't questioning, Counselor. I was intimidating." His lips quirked a little. "Who knows if it'll do any good."

"Intimidating." There were a lot of things she could say to that, including the fact that he certainly was. "Please don't call me 'Counselor.'"

His brows lifted a fraction. "But I don't know your name."

Intimidating, indeed. She was handling this worse than an Assistant District Attorney newly hatched from law school.

"Anne Morden. I used to be with the Public Defender's Office in Philadelphia." She could hardly avoid identifying herself, but some instinct made her want to keep him from knowing where to find her—to find Emilie.

He nodded, but his face gave no clue as to his thoughts. Strength showed in the straight planes and square chin. His hair, worn in an aggressively military cut, was as dark as those chocolate eyes. Even the blue police uniform looked military on him, all sharp creases and crisp lines.

"A Philadelphia lawyer. Around here they say if you want to win, you hire a Philadelphia lawyer." His gaze seemed to sharpen. "So whose battle are you here to win, Ms. Morden? Not Davey Flagler's."

"Davey? No." The boy had been only a preliminary skirmish; they both knew it. For an instant she was tempted to say she represented someone else, but knew that would never work. The plain truth was her only weapon.

"Well, Counselor?"

Her mouth tightened at the implied insult in his use of the title. But one hardly expected police to look kindly on defense attorneys—and most times the feeling was mutual.

"I'm not representing anyone but myself." She glanced down at Emilie, who banged her rattle on the stroller tray. "And my daughter. I'm here because—'' The words stuck in her throat. How could she say this? But she had to.

With a sense that she'd passed the point of no return, she forced the words out. "Because I believe you are Emilie's biological father."

Impassive or not, there was no mistaking the expression that crossed his face as her words penetrated—sheer stupefaction.

Donovan stared at her, shifted the stare to the baby, then back to her. If his eyes had softened slightly when they assessed Emilie, that softness turned to granite when his gaze met hers.

"Lady, you're plain crazy. I've never seen you before in my life."

For an instant Anne was speechless. Then she felt her cheeks color. He thought she meant they...

"No! I mean, I know you haven't." She took a deep breath, willing herself to be calm. If she behaved this way in court, all her clients would be in prison.

His eyes narrowed, fine lines fanning out from them. "Then what do you mean?" The question shot across the desk, and his very stillness spoke of anger raging underneath iron control.

"Emilie..."

As if hearing her name, Emilie chose that moment to burst into wails. She stiffened, thrusting herself backward in the stroller.

Anne bent over her. "Hush, sweetheart." She lifted the baby, standing to hold her on one hip.

"There, it's all right." She bounced her gently. "Don't cry."

The wail turned to a whimper, and Anne dropped a kiss on Emilie's fine, silky hair. Maybe she shouldn't have brought the baby with her, but she couldn't bear the thought of being away from her in this crisis.

The whimpers eased, and Emilie thrust her fingers into her mouth. Anne looked at the man on the other side of the desk, searching vainly for any resemblance to her daughter.

"I didn't put that well." She cradled the baby against her. "I'm not Emilie's birth mother. I'm her foster mother. I'm trying to adopt her."

Donovan shot out of the chair, as if he couldn't be still any longer. He leaned forward, hands planted on the desk.

"Why did you come in here with an accusation like that? What proof do you have?"

"I have the birth mother's statement."

That had to rock him, yet his expression didn't change. "Where is she? Let her make her accusations to my face."

"She can't." Anne's arms tightened protectively around the baby, knowing this was the weakest link in her case, the point at which she was most vulnerable. And Donovan was definitely a man who'd zero in on any vulnerability. "She's dead."

Mitch stared at the woman for a long moment, anger simmering behind the impassive mask he kept in place by sheer force of will. What game was this woman playing? Was this some kind of setup?

"What do you want?"

The abrupt question seemed to throw her. She cradled the baby against her body as if she needed to protect it.

From him. The realization pierced his anger. Protecting was his job, had been since the moment he put on a shield. Assist, protect, defend—the military police code. Nobody needed protecting from him, not unless they'd broken the law.

"You admit it, then? That you're Emilie's father?"

He leaned toward her, resisting the urge to charge around the desk. It was better, much better, to keep the barricade between them.

"I'm not admitting a thing. I want to know what brought you here. Or who."

Something that might have been hope died in her deep-blue eyes. "I told you. The baby's mother said you were the father."

"You also told me she's dead. That makes it pretty convenient to come here with this trumped-up claim."

"Trumped up?" Anger crackled around her. "I certainly didn't make this up. Why would I?"

"You tell me." It was astonishing that his voice was so calm, given the way his mind darted this way and that, trying to make sense of this.

One thing he was sure of—the baby wasn't his. His jaw tightened until it felt about to break. He'd decided a long time ago he wasn't cut out for fatherhood, and he didn't take chances.

"That's ridiculous." Even her hair seemed to spark with anger, as if touching it might shock him. "I came here because I know you're Emilie's father."

His life practically flashed before his eyes as she repeated those words. Everything he'd worked for, the respect he'd enjoyed in the two years since his return—all of it would vanish when her accusation exploded. If the story got out, it wouldn't matter that it wasn't true. By the time it had spread up one side of Main Street and down the other, all the denials in the world wouldn't make it go away.

Those Donovans have always been trouble, that's what people would say. *The apple doesn't fall far from the tree.*

"You're wrong," he said flatly. "I don't know who that child's parents are, but you're not going to get anything out of claiming I'm her father except to cause me a lot of grief."

The idea startled her—he could see it in her eyes. "I didn't come here to create a scandal." She stroked the baby's back, her mouth suddenly vulnerable as she looked at the child.

"Good." He almost believed she meant it, and the thought cut through his anger to some rational part of his mind. He had to start thinking, not reacting. He went around the desk and leaned against it, trying for an ease he didn't feel. "Then why did you come?"

She thought he was capitulating, he could tell. A smile lit her face that almost took his breath away. A man would do a lot for a smile like that.

"All I want is your signature on a parental rights termination so the adoption can go through. Once I have that, Emilie and I will walk out of your life for good."

"That's all?"

She nodded. "You'll never see us again."

"And if I don't sign?"

Her arms tightened around the baby. "I've taken care of Emilie since the day she was born. Her mother wanted me to adopt her. Why would you want to stand in the way?"

They were right where they'd started, and she wouldn't like his answer.

"I don't." He leaned forward, bridged the gap between them and touched the baby's cheek. It earned him a smile. "She's a cute kid. But she's not mine."

She turned away abruptly, bending to slide the baby into the stroller. Emilie fussed for an instant, until Anne put a stuffed toy in front of her.

When she straightened, her eyes were chips of blue ice. "I'm not trying to trap you into anything."

"I'd like to believe that, but it doesn't change anything. I'm still not her father."

She gave an impatient shrug. "I've told you the mother named you."

"You haven't even told me who she is. Or how you fit into this story." He was finally starting to think like a cop. It was about time. "Look." He tried to find the words that would gain him some cooperation. "I believe I'm not this child's father. You believe I am. Seems to me, two reasonable adults can sit down and get everything out in the open. How do you expect me to react when an accusation like this comes out of nowhere?"

He could see her assess his words from every angle.

"All right," she said finally. "You know what my interest is. I want to adopt Emilie."

There had to be a lot more to the story than that, but he'd settle for the bare bones at the moment. "And the mother? Who was she? What happened to her?"

He gripped the edge of the desk behind him. He probably shouldn't fire questions at her, but he couldn't help it.

She frowned. Maybe she was editing her words. "Her mother's name was Tina Mallory. Now do you remember her?"

The name landed unpleasantly between them. *Tina Mallory.* He wanted to be able to say he'd never heard of her, but he couldn't, because the name echoed with some faint familiarity. He'd heard it before, but where? And how much of his sense of recognition did Anne Morden guess?

"How am I supposed to have known her?"

"She lived here in Bedford Creek at one time."

In Bedford Creek. If she'd lived here, why didn't he remember her? "I'm afraid it still doesn't ring any bells."

That was only half-right. It rang a bell; he just didn't know why.

"Doesn't the police chief know everyone in a town this small?" Her eyebrows arched.

Before he could come up with an answer, the telephone rang, and seconds later Wanda Clay bellowed, "Chief! Call for you."

Anne's silky black hair brushed her shoulders as she glanced toward the door.

He reached for the phone. "Excuse me. I have to do the job the town pays me for."

He picked up the receiver, turned away from her. It was a much-needed respite. He let Mrs. Bennett's complaint about her neighbors drift through his mind. He didn't need to listen, often as he'd heard the same story. What he did need to do was think. He had to find some way to put off Anne Morden until he figured out who Tina Mallory was.

"We'll take care of it, Mrs. Bennett, I promise." A few more soothing phrases, and he hung up.

Anne looked as if she wanted to tap her foot with impatience. "Now can we discuss this?"

The phone rang again, giving him the perfect excuse. "Not without interruption, as you can see. Where are you staying?"

She stiffened. "I hadn't intended to be here that long. Why can't we finish this now?"

"Because I have a job to do." His mind twisted around obstacles. He'd also better run a check on Anne Morden before he did another thing. He at least had to make sure she was who she claimed to be. "How about getting together this evening?"

"This evening?" She made it sound like an eternity. "It's a three-hour drive back to Philadelphia, and Emilie's tired already."

He was tempted to say *Take it or leave it,* but now was not the time for ultimatums. It might come to that, but not if he could make her see she was wrong.

"Look, this is too important to rush. Why don't you plan to stay over?"

"I'd like to get home tonight."

Her tone had softened a little. At least she was considering his suggestion.

"Isn't this more important?" He pushed the advantage.

She looked at the baby, then back at him, and nodded slowly. "It's worth staying, if I can get this cleared up once and for all."

Mitch took a piece of notepaper from the desk and scribbled an address on it. "The Willows is a bed-and-breakfast. Kate Cavendish will take good care of you."

He considered it a minor triumph when she accepted the paper.

"All right." Maybe she'd anticipated all along that this wouldn't be settled in a hurry. "If that's what it takes, Emilie and I will stay over. When can I expect to see you?"

He glanced at his watch, reviewing all he'd need to accomplish. "Say between six and seven?"

She nodded hesitantly, as if wary of agreeing to anything he said. "I'll see you then."

He didn't breathe until she and the baby were gone. Then it felt as if he hadn't breathed the whole time she'd been there. Well, the news she'd brought would rattle anyone.

Just how much stock could he put in what Anne Morden said? He leaned back in his chair, considering.

It didn't take much effort to picture her sitting across from him. Cool composure—that was the first thing he'd noticed about her. She'd reminded him of every smart, savvy attorney he'd ever locked horns with, except that she was beautiful. Hair as silky and black as a ripple of satin, skin like creamy porcelain, eyes blue as a mountain lake.

Beautiful. Also way out of his class, with her designer clothes and superior air.

Well, beautiful or not, Ms. Anne Morden had to be checked out. He hoped he could find some ammunition with which to defend himself, before she blew his life apart.

He reached for the phone.

Chapter Two

Anne put a light blanket over Emilie, who slept soundly in the crib Mrs. Cavendish had installed in the bedroom of the suite. Nothing, it seemed, was too much trouble for a friend of Chief Donovan's. No one else was staying at the bed-and-breakfast now, and Mrs. Cavendish—Kate, she'd insisted Anne call her—had given them a bedroom with an adjoining sitting room on the second floor of the rambling Victorian house.

The rooms were country quaint, furnished with mismatched antiques that looked as if they'd always sat just where they did now. The quilt on the brass bed appeared to be handmade, and dried flowers filled the pottery basin on the oak washstand. A ghost of last summer's fragrance wafted from them.

She would have enjoyed the place in any other

circumstances; it might have been a welcome retreat. But not when her baby's future was at stake.

She had to get herself under control before her next unsettling meeting with Mitch Donovan. This afternoon—well, this afternoon she could have done better, couldn't she?

Her stomach still clenched with tension when she pictured Donovan's frowning face. She still felt the power with which he'd rejected her words.

She shouldn't have been surprised. A man in his position had a lot to lose. The chief of police in a small town couldn't afford a scandal.

The sitting room window overlooked the street, which wound its way uphill from the river in a series of jogs. Bedford Creek was dwarfed by the mountain ridges that hemmed it in. What did people in this village think of their police chief? And what would they think of him if they knew he'd had an affair with a young girl, leaving her pregnant?

They might close ranks against the stranger who brought such an accusation. A chill shivered down her spine.

If Mitch Donovan persisted in his denials, what option did she have? Making the whole business public would only hurt all three of them. But if she didn't get his signature on the document, she'd live in constant fear.

What was she going to do? Panic shot through her. She pressed her hands against the wide windowsill, trying to force the fear down.

Turn to the Lord, child. She could practically hear Helen's warm, rich voice say the words, and her fear ebbed a little at the thought of her friend.

Helen Wells had introduced her to the Lord, just as simply as if she were introducing one friend to another. Until Anne walked into the Faith House shelter Helen ran, looking for a client who'd missed a hearing, religion had been nothing but form. It had been a ritual her parents had insisted on twice a year—the times when everyone went to the appropriate church, wearing the appropriate clothing.

They'd have found nothing appropriate about Faith House or its director, Helen Wells—the tall, elegant woman's embracing warmth for everyone who crossed her threshold was outside their experience. But Anne had found a friend there, and a faith she'd never expected to encounter. Helen's wisdom had sustained her faith through the difficult season of her husband's death.

Not that she was under any illusion her faith was mature. *God's not finished with you yet,* Helen would say, wrapping Anne in the same warm embrace she extended to every lost soul and runaway kid who wandered into her shelter. *The good Lord has plenty for you to learn, girl. But you have to listen.*

God could help in this situation with Donovan. She had to believe that, somehow.

But maybe believing it would be easier if she had the kind of faith Helen did.

I'm trying, Lord. You know I'm trying.

A police car came slowly down the street and pulled to the curb in front of the bed-and-breakfast. She let the curtain fall behind her, her heart giving an awkward *thump*. Mitch Donovan was here.

In a moment she heard footsteps in the hall beneath, heard Kate greeting him—fondly, it seemed. Well, of course. Bedford Creek was his home. Anne was the stranger here, and she had to remember that.

By the time he knocked, Anne had donned her calm, professional manner. But after she opened the door, her coolness began to unravel. He still wore the uniform that seemed almost a part of him, and his dark gaze was intent and determined.

"Chief Donovan. Come in."

He nodded, moving through the doorway as assuredly as if he were walking into his office. The small room suddenly filled with his masculine presence.

It's the uniform, she told herself, fingers tightening on the brass knob as she closed the door. That official uniform would rattle anyone, especially combined with the sheer rock-solid nature of the man wearing it.

"Getting settled?" His firm mouth actually curved in a smile. "I see Kate gave you her best room."

Apparently he hoped to get this meeting off to a more pleasant start than the last one. Well, that was what she wanted, too. *You need his cooperation,* she reminded herself. *For Emilie's sake.*

"Any friend of Mitch's deserves the nicest one— I think that's what she said." Anne couldn't help it if her tone sounded a bit dry.

He walked to the window, glanced out at the street below, then turned back to her. "Kate said you took a walk around town."

The small talk was probably as much an effort for him as for her. She longed to burst into the crucial questions, but held them back.

Cooperate, remember? That's how to get what you want.

"I stopped by the pharmacy to pick up some extra diapers for the baby. The pharmacist already knew I'd been to see you." That had astonished her. "Your dispatcher must work fast."

The source of the information had to be the dispatcher. Mitch Donovan certainly wouldn't advertise her presence.

He grimaced. "Wanda loves to spread news. And it is a small town, except during tourist season."

"Tourist season?"

He gestured out the window, and she moved a little reluctantly to stand next to him.

"Take a look at those mountains. Our only claim to fame."

The sun slipped behind a thickly forested ridge, painting the sky with red. The village seemed wedged into the narrow valley, as if forced to climb the slope from the river because it couldn't spread out. The river glinted at the valley floor, reflecting the last of the light.

"It is beautiful."

"Plenty of people are willing to pay for this view, and the Chamber of Commerce is happy to let them."

"I guess that explains the number of bed-and-breakfasts. And the shops." She had noticed the assortment of small stores that lined the main street—candles, pottery, stained glass. "Bedford Creek must have an artistic population."

"Don't let any of the old-timers hear you say that." The tiny lines at the corners of his eyes crinkled as his face relaxed in the first genuine smile she'd seen. "They leave such things to outsiders."

"Outsiders." That seemed to echo what she'd been thinking. "You mean people like me?"

He shook his head. "They make a distinction between outsiders and visitors. Outsiders are people like the candle-makers and potters who want to turn the place into an artists' colony. The old guard understands that, whether they approve or not. But visiting lawyers—visiting lawyers must be here for a reason."

"So that's why everyone I passed looked twice."

He shrugged. "In the off-season, strangers are always news. Especially a woman and baby who come to call on the bachelor police chief." His mouth twisted a little wryly on the words.

She'd clearly underestimated the power of the grapevine in a small town. But his apparent concern about rumors might work to her advantage.

"No one will know why I'm here from me. I promise."

She almost put her hand out, as if to shake on it, and then changed her mind. She didn't want friendship from the man, just cooperation. Just his signature, that was all.

"Thanks."

He took a step closer...close enough that she could feel his warmth and smell the faint, musky aroma of shaving lotion. Her pulse thumped, startling her, and she took an impulsive step back, trying to deny the warmth that swept over her.

She must be crazy. He was tough, arrogant, controlling—everything she most disliked in a man. Even if she had been remotely interested in a relationship—which she wasn't—it wouldn't be with someone like him.

But her breathing had quickened, and his dark eyes were intent on hers, as if seeing something he hadn't noticed before. She felt heat flood her cheeks.

Business, she reminded herself. She'd better get down to business. It was the only thing they had in common.

"Have you thought about signing the papers?" She knew in an instant she shouldn't have blurted it out, but her carefully prepared speech had deserted her. In her plans for this meeting, she hadn't considered that she might be rattled at being alone with him.

Whatever friendliness had been in his eyes vanished. "I'd like to talk about this." His uncompromising tone told her the situation wasn't going to turn suddenly easy. "About the woman, Tina."

"Do you remember her now?" She didn't mean the words to sound sarcastic, but they probably did. She bit her lip. There was just no good way to discuss this.

"No." Luckily he seemed to take the question at face value. "Do you know when she was here?"

"Emilie was born in June. Tina said she'd been here the previous summer and stayed through the fall." He could count the months as easily as she could.

He frowned. "Tourist season. They come right through the autumn colors. That means there are plenty of transient workers in town. People who show up in late spring, get jobs, then leave again the end of October." He shook his head. "Impossible to remember them all or keep track of them while they're here."

She'd left her bag on the pie-crust table. She flipped it open and took out the photograph she'd brought. A wave of sadness flooded her as she looked at the young face.

"This was Tina." She held it out to him.

He took the photo and stood frowning down at it, straight brows drawn over his eyes. She should be watching for a spark of recognition, she thought, instead of noticing how his uniform shirt fit his broad shoulders, not a wrinkle marring its perfection. The crease in his navy trousers looked sharp enough to cut paper, and his shoes shone as if they'd been polished moments before.

He looked up finally, his gaze finding hers without the antagonism she half expected. "How did you meet her?"

She bit back a sharp response. "Isn't it more pertinent to ask how *you* met her?"

His mouth hardened in an already hard face. "All right. I recognize her now that I've seen the picture. But I never knew her name. And I certainly didn't have an affair with her."

That was progress, of a sort. If she could manage not to sound as if she judged him, maybe he'd move toward being honest with her.

She tried to keep her tone neutral. "How did you know her?"

"She worked at the café that summer." He frowned, as if remembering. "I eat a lot of meals there, so she waited on me. Chatted, the way waitresses do with regulars. But I didn't run into her anywhere else."

His dark gaze met hers, challenging her to argue. "Your turn. How did you get to know her?"

"She answered an ad I'd put on the bulletin board at the corner market. She wanted to rent a room in my house."

His eyebrows went up at that. "Sorry, Counselor, but you don't look as if you need to take in boarders."

"I didn't do it for the money." She clipped off the words. Her instincts warned her not to give too much away to this man, but if she wanted his cooperation she'd have to appear willing to answer his questions. "My husband had died a few months earlier, and I'd taken a leave from my job. I'd been rattling around in a place too big for one person. The roomer was just going to be temporary, until I found a buyer for the house."

"How long ago was that?" It was a cop's question, snapped at her as if she were a suspect.

"A little over a year." She tried not to let his manner rattle her. "I knew she was pregnant, of course, but I didn't know she had a heart condition. I'm not sure even she knew at first. The doctors said she never should have gotten pregnant."

"What about her family?"

"She said she didn't have anyone." Tina had seemed just as lonely as Anne had been. Maybe that was what had drawn them together. "We became friends. And then when she had to be hospitalized— well, I guess I felt responsible for her. She didn't have anyone else. When Emilie was born, Tina's condition worsened. I took charge of the baby. Tina never came home from the hospital."

His strong face was guarded. "Is that when she supposedly told you about me?"

She nodded. "She talked about the time she spent in Bedford Creek, about the man she loved, the man who fathered Emilie."

He was so perfectly still that he might have been a statue, except for the tiny muscle that pulsed at his temple. "And if I tell you it was a mistake— that she couldn't have meant me...?"

"Look, I'm not here to prosecute you." Why couldn't he see that? "I'm not judging you. I just want your signature on the papers. That's all."

"You didn't answer me." He took a step closer, and she could feel the intensity under his iron exterior. "What if I tell you it was a mistake?"

It was all slipping away, getting out of her control. "How could it be a mistake? Everything she said fits you, no one else."

He seized on that. "Fits me? I thought you said she named me."

She took a deep breath, trying to stay in control of the situation. "While she was ill, she talked a lot about...about the man she fell in love with. About the town. Then, when we knew she wasn't going to get better, we made plans for Emilie's adoption." She looked at him, willing him to understand. "I've been taking care of Emilie practically since the day she was born. I love her. Tina knew that. She knew I needed the father's permission, too, but she never said the name until the end."

She shivered a little, recalling the scene. Tina,

slipping in and out of consciousness, finally saying the name *Mitch Donovan.* "Why would she lie?"

"I don't know." His mouth clamped firmly on the words. "I'm sorry, sorry about all of it. But I'm not the father of her baby."

She glared at him, wanting to shake the truth out of him. But it was no use. It would be about as effective as shaking a rock.

"You don't believe me." He made it a simple statement of fact.

"No." There seemed little point in saying anything else.

Mitch's jaw clamped painfully tight. This woman was so sure she was right that it would take a bulldozer to move her. Somehow he had to crack open that closed mind of hers enough for her to admit doubt.

"Isn't it possible you misunderstood?" He struggled, trying to come up with a theory to explain the unexplainable. "If she was as sick as you say, maybe her mind wandered."

For the first time some of the certainty faded in her eyes. She stared beyond him, as if focusing on something painful in the past.

"I don't think so." Her gaze met his, troubled, as if she were trying to be fair. "We'd been talking about the adoption. Certainly she knew what I was asking her."

"Look, I don't have an explanation for this." He

spread his hands wide. "All I can say is what I've already told you. I knew the girl slightly, and she was here at the right time. I don't know how to prove a negative, but I never had an affair with her, and I did not father her child."

Something hardened inside him as he said the words. He didn't have casual affairs—not that it was any of Anne Morden's business. And he certainly wasn't cut out for fatherhood. If there was anything his relationship with his own father had taught him, it was that the Donovan men didn't make decent fathers. The whole town knew that.

"If you were to sign the parental rights termination…" she began.

He lifted an eyebrow. "Is that really what you want, Counselor? You want me to lie?"

Her soft mouth could look uncommonly stubborn. "Would it be a lie?"

"Yes." That much he knew. And he could only see one way to prove it in the face of Anne's persistence and the mother's dying statement. "I suggest we put it to the test. A blood test."

That must have occurred to her. It was the obvious solution. And her quick nod told him she'd thought of it.

"Fine. Is there a lab in town?"

"Not here." He didn't even need to consider that. "We can't have it done in Bedford Creek." He hoped he didn't sound as horrified at the thought as he felt.

"Why not?" The suspicion was back in her eyes.

"You've obviously never lived in a small town. If the three of us show up at the clinic for a paternity test, the town will know about it before the needle hits my skin."

"That bad?" She almost managed a smile.

"Believe me, it's that bad. Rebecca Forrester, the doctor's assistant, wouldn't say a word. But the receptionist talks as much as my dispatcher."

"The nearest town where they have the facilities—"

"I'd rather go to Philadelphia, if you don't mind." She shouldn't. After all, that was her home turf.

"That's fine with me, but isn't it a little out of the way for you?"

"Far enough that I won't be worried about running into anyone who'll carry the news back to Bedford Creek." It was a small world, all right, but surely not that small. "I have a friend who's on the staff of a city hospital. He can make sure we have it done quickly. And discreetly." Though what Brett would say to him at this request, he didn't want to imagine.

"This friend of yours—" she began.

"Brett's a good physician. He wouldn't jeopardize his career by tinkering with test results."

She seemed to look at it from every angle before she nodded. "All right. Tomorrow?"

"Tomorrow, it is."

He forced his muscles to relax. Tomorrow, if luck was with him, a simple screening would prove he couldn't possibly be the child's father. Anne Morden would take her baby and walk back out of his life as quickly as she'd walked in.

He should be feeling relief. He definitely shouldn't be feeling regret at the thought of never seeing her again.

Chapter Three

Anne made the turn from the Schulkyll Express-
way toward center city and glanced across at her
passenger. Mitch stared straight ahead, hands flexed
on his knees. He wore khaki slacks and a button-
down shirt today, his leather jacket thrown into the
back seat, but even those clothes had a military aura.

Nothing in his posture indicated any uncertainty
about her driving, but she was nevertheless sure that
he'd rather be behind the wheel.

Well, that was too bad. Riding to Philadelphia
together had been his idea, after all. He'd said his
car was in the shop, and if she thought he wanted
to drive the police car on an errand like this, she'd
better think again. He'd ride down with her and get
a rental car for the return.

The trip had been accomplished mostly in silence,

except for the occasional chirps from Emilie in her car seat. Mitch probably had no desire to chat, anyway, and her thoughts had twisted all the way down the turnpike.

Was she doing the right thing? A blood test was the obvious solution, of course, and she'd recommended it often enough to clients. She just hadn't anticipated the need in this situation. She'd assumed a man in Mitch's position, faced with the results of a casual fling, would be only too happy to sign the papers and put his mistake behind him.

But it hadn't worked out that way, and his willingness to undergo the blood test lent credence to his denials. She was almost tempted to believe him.

What was she thinking? He had to be Emilie's father, didn't he? Tina would certainly know, and Tina had said so.

They passed a sign directing them to the hospital, and her nerves tightened. Maybe she shouldn't have agreed to let Mitch make the arrangements, but it sounded sensible, the way he had put it. They could be assured speed and secrecy through his connection.

"I hope your friend is ready for us." She glanced at her watch. Dr. Brett Elliot had given them an afternoon appointment, and they should be right on time.

"He'll be there." Mitch's granite expression cracked in a reminiscent smile. "In high school Brett was always the one with the late assignment and the joke that made the teacher laugh so she didn't penalize him. But medical school reformed him. You'd hardly guess he was once the class clown.''

Somehow the title didn't sound very reassuring. She glanced sideways at Mitch, registering again his size and strength. "Let me guess. You must have been the class's star athlete.''

He shrugged. "Something like that, I guess.''

The hospital parking garage loomed on her right. Anne pulled in, the sandwich she'd had for lunch turning into a lead ball in her stomach. In an hour or two, she might know for sure about Emilie's father.

Mitch's friend had said he'd be waiting at the lab desk. Actually, he seemed to be leaning on it. Unruly hair the color of antique gold tumbled into his eyes as he laughed down at the woman behind the desk. So this was the boy who'd charmed everyone—all grown up and still doing it, apparently.

"Mitch!" He crossed the room in a few long strides and pumped Mitch's hand. "Good to see you, guy. It's been too long.''

Brett's face, open and smiling, contrasted with Mitch's closed, reserved look, but nothing could disguise the affection between them. Mitch clapped him on the shoulder before turning to Anne and introducing her.

Brett gave her the same warm grin he'd been giving the woman at the desk, but she thought she read wariness in his green eyes. Then he turned to Emilie, and all reservation vanished.

"Hey, there, pretty girl. What's your name?"

"This is Emilie."

"What a little sweetheart." He tickled Emilie's chin, and even the eight-month-old baby responded to him with a shy smile and a tilt of her head.

Brett gestured toward the orange vinyl chairs lining the empty waiting room. "Since we've got the place to ourselves, let's have a chat about what we're going to do."

The woman behind the desk muttered an excuse and disappeared into the adjoining room. Anne took a seat, Emilie on her lap, and vague misgivings floated through her mind. *These are Mitch's arrangements,* she cautioned herself. *This is Mitch's friend.*

Brett pulled his chair around to face them. "The first step is to do a preliminary screening of blood type and Rh factors. We'll be able to give you those results right away."

"They're not definitive in establishing paternity." She didn't mean to sound critical, but she'd handled enough cases to know it usually went farther than that.

"Not entirely." Brett didn't seem put off by her lawyer-like response. "But there are some combinations that can exclude the possibility of paternity, and that's what we look for first."

Another objection stirred in Anne's mind. "Don't you need the mother's blood type to do that?"

"Yes, well, actually I got the information from the hospital where Emilie was born."

He exchanged a quick glance with Mitch. Obviously they'd arranged that when they talked, too.

"My military records show my blood type." Mitch frowned. "We could have gotten them."

"This is faster than waiting for the military to send something," Brett said, before Anne could voice an objection. "And in a legal matter, we can't just rely on your word."

Mitch's mouth tightened, but he nodded.

"Okay, so if the screening rules Mitch out," the doctor continued, "we stop there. If it doesn't, that still means he's one of maybe a million people who could be the father. So we go to DNA testing at that point. It takes longer, but it'll establish paternity beyond any doubt."

Emilie stirred restlessly on Anne's lap, as if to remind her she'd had a long, upsetting couple of days. Anne stroked her head. "I understand."

"Let's get on with it." Mitch seemed ready for action, and she half expected him to push up his sleeve on the spot.

"Fine." Brett started toward the laboratory door.

Ready or not. Anne picked up Emilie and followed him, suddenly breathless. She'd know something, maybe soon.

Mitch's stony expression didn't change in the

least when the technician plunged a needle into his hard-muscled arm. Emilie wasn't so stoic. She stiffened, head thumping hard against Anne's chest, and let out an anguished wail that tore into Anne's heart.

"Hey, little girl." Mitch's voice was astonishingly gentle. One large hand wrapped around the baby's flailing foot. "It'll be over in a second, honest."

When the needle was gone, Emilie's sobs subsided, but Anne didn't have any illusions. The baby was overtired and overstimulated, and she desperately needed to have her dinner and go to sleep. That wouldn't hurt her mother any, either.

"It's all right, darling." She stroked Emilie's fine blond hair. "We'll go home soon."

Brett nodded. "This won't take long. Make yourselves comfortable in the waiting room, and I'll bring you some coffee."

A few minutes later they were back in the same chairs they'd occupied earlier. Anne tried to balance a wiggling Emilie while digging for a bottle of juice in the diaper bag. The juice remained elusive.

"Here, let me hold her." Before she could object, Mitch took the baby from her. He bounced Emilie on his knees, rumpling the knife-sharp crease, his strong hands supporting the baby's back.

The ache between Anne's shoulder blades eased. She watched Mitch with the baby, realizing the ache had just shifted location to her heart. If Mitch was Emilie's father...

She bent over the diaper bag to hide the tears that clouded her eyes. Ridiculous to feel them. Nothing had changed. She blinked rapidly and fished the juice bottle out.

"I'll take her now." She flipped the cap off and dropped it in the bag.

Mitch shook his head and reached for the bottle. "Give yourself a break for a few minutes. I can manage this."

She leaned back, watching as he shifted Emilie's position and plopped the nipple into her mouth.

"You didn't learn that in...the Army, was it?"

He nodded. "Military Police. Matter of fact, I did. A couple of my buddies had families."

She thought she heard a note of censure in his voice. "You have something against that?"

His eyes met hers, startled, and then he shrugged. "Up to them. I just never figured family mixed very well with military police work."

Emilie snuggled against him, fingers curling and uncurling on the bottle, eyes beginning to droop.

"I see you hung around enough to learn how to give a bottle."

His face relaxed in a smile. The effect was startling, warming his whole countenance and demanding an answering smile she couldn't suppress.

"Not too difficult. Besides, I could always give the babies back if they got fussy."

"Of course."

Something hardened in her at the words. The

three of them might look, to the casual observer, like a family. That observer couldn't begin to guess how skewed that impression was.

Emilie had fallen asleep in Mitch's arms by the time Brett pushed through the door, a clipboard in his hand. Anne inhaled sharply and saw Mitch's already erect posture stiffen even more.

"Well?" Mitch's voice rasped. "What's the verdict?"

Brett's green eyes were troubled. "Skipping all the technical details, the bottom line is the tests don't exclude you, Mitch. Your blood type means you could possibly be the father."

"Me and a million other guys," he snapped.

Anne's mouth tightened. He'd obviously been hoping against hope he hadn't been caught. Maybe now he'd give up this pose of innocence and sign the papers. But she had to show him she'd keep pressing.

"About the DNA test—" she pinned Brett with her gaze "—I'd like it sent to McKay Labs. I've dealt with them before. And I want a copy of the results sent directly to me."

Brett blinked. "That'll need Mitch's permission."

"You've got it." Mitch moved, and Emilie woke. Her whimper quickly turned into a full-fledged cry.

Brett looked ready to escape. "Expect the results in three to four weeks, then."

Anne nodded goodbye, trying to reach for the diaper bag and her crying child at the same time. "Let me have her."

Mitch handed over the baby.

"There, sweetheart, it's all right." She rocked the baby against her, but Emilie was beyond comforting. She reared back in Anne's arms, wails increasing.

Mitch picked up the diaper bag. "You can't drive home alone with her in that state." He took her arm. "Come on. I'll drive you and then call a cab."

She wanted to protest, but Emilie's sobs shattered her will. She nodded, letting him guide her from the room.

The baby's wails seemed to fry Mitch's brain as he followed Anne's directions through the city streets to a high-rise apartment building. He needed to think this whole thing through, but thought proved impossible at the moment. Who would imagine one small baby could make that much noise?

He took a deep breath as the cry reached a decibel level that had to be against the law inside a small car. Okay, he could handle this. It was no worse than artillery fire, was it?

Besides, it would soon be over. He'd deposit them at Anne's and call a cab. He'd be back in Bedford Creek in a few hours, and the only contact he'd have with Anne Morden and her baby would be when the DNA test came back, proving he hadn't fathered this child.

A padded, mirrored elevator whooshed them

swiftly to the tenth floor. He took the baby, wincing at her cries, while Anne unlocked the door. He wanted only to hand her back and get out of there.

She scooped the baby into her arms as the door swung open, and her eyes met his. "This may not be the best time, but I think we should talk the situation over, if you don't mind waiting while I get the baby settled." She managed a half smile. "It won't take as long as you might think. She's so exhausted, she's going to crash as soon as she's been fed."

He pushed down the desire to flee, nodded, and followed her into the apartment. Anne disappeared into the back with the baby, and he sank onto the couch, wondering when the ringing in his ears would stop.

Anne had sold the house she'd talked about and moved here with the baby. He'd found that out in the quick background check he'd run. He glanced around. Expensively casual—that was the only way to describe her apartment. Chintz couches, a soft plush carpet, a wall of books on built-in shelves with what was probably a state-of-the-art entertainment center discreetly hidden behind closed doors—all said money. Assistant public defenders didn't make enough to support this life-style, but there was wealth in her family. This woman was really out of his league.

No question of that, anyway. All she wanted from

him was his signature on the parental rights termination—not friendship, certainly nothing more.

Sometime in the last twenty-four hours he'd given up any thought that Anne was somehow attempting to frame him. No, all she wanted was to safeguard her child.

Unfortunately the one thing she wanted, he couldn't give her. Someone else had dated the unfortunate Tina; someone else had fathered her child. But who? And why on earth had the girl said his name? The answers, if they could be found at all, must lie in Bedford Creek.

The baby's cries from the back of the apartment ceased abruptly. Anne must have put some food in Emilie's mouth.

He got up, paced to the window, then paced back. What did Anne want to talk to him about? What was there left to say?

He sat back down on the couch, sinking into its comfortable depths, and reached automatically for the book on the lamp table. A Bible. It nestled into his hand, and he flipped it open to the dedication page. *To my new sister in Christ from Helen.* The date was only two years ago.

Anne came back into the room, her step light and quick. She glanced questioningly at the Bible in his hand, and he closed it and put it back where he'd found it.

"She settled down, did she?"

"Out like a light."

Anne sat in the chair across from him. Her dark hair curled around a face that was lightly flushed, probably from bending over the crib.

"You're probably as beat as she is by this time." She'd put in a couple of high-stress days, driving all the way with a baby, and on a mission like this.

"I could sleep a day or two. But Emilie won't let me."

She leaned forward and her hair brushed her shoulders, moving like a living thing. He had an insane desire to reach out, let it curl around his fingers, use it to draw her close to him.

Whoa, back off. Of all the inappropriate things he could be feeling right now, that was probably the worst.

"You wanted to talk."

"Yes." She nailed him with those deep blue eyes. "I hoped that you might be ready to sign the papers now."

He should have seen it coming. She still wanted what she'd wanted all along, and the inconclusive blood test results had just given her another bit of leverage. But it wasn't going to work.

"I know you don't believe this, but I never went out with Tina Mallory. I did not father her child." He took a breath, hoping he sounded calm.

She raised her chin stubbornly. "Then how do you explain Tina's words?"

"I can't. But there has to be an explanation somewhere. Someone in Bedford Creek must remember

Tina, must know who she dated that summer. So while we're waiting for the DNA results, I'll do a little quiet investigating.''

Her hands twisted involuntarily, as if she were pushing his words away. He couldn't blame her. She had what must seem to her to be incontrovertible proof of his guilt. All he could do was continue to protest his innocence.

''Bottom line is, I'm not going to sign anything that says I'm that child's parent. I can't, because it's not true. In three or four weeks, you'll know that as well as I do. Maybe by then I'll be able to point you in the right direction.''

''I don't want my private business splashed all over Bedford Creek.''

''Believe me, it's in my interest to keep it quiet even more than it is yours. I'll be discreet. But I'm going to start looking at this problem like a cop.''

Her eyebrows went up at that. ''Funny, I thought you always had.''

He reminded himself that cops and defense attorneys went together like cats and dogs. ''Look, Counselor, I am what I am.'' Her sarcasm had effectively doused that spurt of longing to hold her, which was just as well. He stood, picking up his jacket. ''I'll be on my way now. I don't suppose we'll see each other again.''

''I'm afraid you're wrong about that.'' She stood, too, her gaze locked on his.

He gave an exasperated sigh. ''You're assuming

that in three or four weeks you'll have proof I fathered Emilie. I know you're wrong.''

''Actually, that isn't what I was thinking.'' She took an audible breath, as if building up to saying something she knew he wasn't going to like. ''Emilie and I aren't staying here. We're going back to Bedford Creek until the results come in.''

''What?'' He could only stare at her. ''Why? Why on earth would you want to do that?''

''You're right about one thing—the answers have to be in Bedford Creek. That's where Tina became pregnant. That's where the truth is. I can't just sit here and wonder for the next month. I need to find out, no matter what.''

''After the results come—'' he began.

She was already shaking her head. ''I'm supposed to have a hearing on the adoption in a little over a month. Before then I have to resolve this, once and for all. And that means I'm coming to Bedford Creek.''

He lifted an eyebrow skeptically. ''Don't you mean you want to keep an eye on me?''

A faint flush warmed her smooth skin. ''Let's say I have a high respect for the power of a police uniform. I don't want to see it used against me.''

He fought down the urge to defend himself. If a man found it necessary to defend his honor, it must be in question. He took a careful step back.

''No point in my telling you not to worry about that, is there?''

She shook her head. "I won't interfere. You can pretend I'm not even there."

"Now that I can't do." He smiled grimly at her perplexed look. "You're forgetting—people in Bedford Creek already know you and Emilie came to see me. They're probably speculating right this minute about where we are today. You can't come back and pretend we don't know each other, not in a small town."

"I'll say I'm there on vacation. You told me Bedford Creek is a tourist town. My presence doesn't have to have anything to do with you."

Obviously she hadn't thought this far ahead. "Nobody would believe that. If you come back, we'll have to keep up the illusion of friendship. And if we're both going to be looking into what happened when Tina lived there, we'd better figure out a way to cooperate on this, or at least not step on each other's toes."

He could see just how unpalatable she found that, and at some level it grated on his pride. He wasn't that hard to take, was he? It wasn't as if he were asking her to pretend a romantic interest in him.

Her eyes met his, and he could read the determination there. "I suppose you're right. You know a lot more about your town than I do. But I'm still coming. So that means we're in this together, for as long as it takes."

Chapter Four

"Now let me help you with that." Kate Cavendish took the bundle of diapers from Anne's arms before she could object. "Believe me, I remember how much you need to bring when you're traveling with a baby."

"I can manage…"

But Kate was already hustling up the front steps to The Willows, white curls glistening in the late winter sunshine. She propped the door open with an iron doorstop in the shape of a cat, then hurried inside. Anne lifted Emilie from the car seat.

It was silly, she supposed, to be made uncomfortable by so much open friendliness, but she just wasn't used to it. She could only hope Kate's enthusiastic welcome wasn't because the woman thought Anne was here to see Mitch.

That was ridiculous. It wasn't as if they'd returned together. She'd taken two days to organize this trip. Surely she could take a brief vacation in Bedford Creek without the whole town jumping to conclusions about why she was here.

Kate was probably just delighted to have paying guests at this time of the year. No matter how many tourists might show up in the summer, early March was clearly a quiet time in Bedford Creek. She glanced up at the mountain ridge that cut off the sky. It was sere and brown, its leafless trees defining its bones. She shivered a little.

"Here we go, sweetheart," she said to Emilie. "We'll just pop you in the crib while Mommy unloads the car, all right?"

Emilie wiggled, her arms flailing in the pink snowsuit. After three hours in the car, she was only too ready to practice her new crawling skills. She wouldn't be pleased at the crib, no matter how enticing Anne made it sound.

As they reached the center hall of the Victorian, Kate hurried down the winding staircase. The colors of the stained-glass window on the landing tinged her hair, and a smile lit her bright-blue eyes at the sight of the baby.

"Oh, let me take her, please. I'd just love to hold her." Kate held out her hands.

Emilie leaned her head against Anne's shoulder for a moment, considering, and then smiled, her chubby hands opening toward the woman. Emilie had apparently decided anyone who looked like Mrs. Santa Claus had to be a friend.

"You little sweetheart." Kate settled the baby on her hip with the ease of long practice. "We're going to be great friends while you're here, I can just tell."

"Thank you, Kate." Anne touched Emilie's cheek lightly. "I appreciate the help. It will just take me a few minutes to unload."

"Take your time." Kate carried the baby toward the wide archway into the front parlor. "We'll get acquainted. I'm surprised Mitch isn't here to get you settled. He's always so helpful to his friends."

Was that a question in Kate's voice? Maybe this was her chance to refute any rumors the woman had heard. Or started, for that matter. She moved to the archway.

"Mitch and I aren't that close. He probably didn't even know when we were arriving."

"Oh, I'm sure he did." Kate turned from the breakfront cabinet, where she was showing Emilie a collection of china birds. "He keeps track of things. And when his old Army friend's widow comes to visit...well, you can just be sure he'd keep track of that." Kate's round cheeks, like two red apples, plumped in a smile. "It's so nice that you could keep in touch."

"Old Army friend...how did you—" *Leap to that conclusion*—that was what she was thinking, but it hardly seemed polite to say so. She'd mentioned that she was a widow when she'd checked in the first time. Kate seemed to have embroidered the rest.

"Wanda had all sorts of ideas about why you were here." Kate tickled Emilie's chin. "I told her, 'Count on it, that'll be why. Mitch's friends from the service have dropped by four or five times since he's been back in Bedford Creek. That's why Anne and her baby are here, too.'"

Mitch clearly knew his town a lot better than Anne did. She owed him an apology for thinking he was wrong about the stir her presence would create. As he'd said, she needed a reason to be here.

Anne opened her mouth and closed it again. What exactly could she say? Wanda, the dispatcher, had probably floated some much more colorful theories about Anne's visit. If Anne denied Kate's story, she'd just fuel the curiosity. She certainly wasn't going to lie about it, but maybe the safest thing was to say nothing and let them think what they wanted.

"I'm sure Mitch is busy." She settled on non-committal. "I probably won't see much of him while we're here."

Kate swung around again, eyebrows going up in surprise. "Not see much of him? Well, of course you will. After all, his house is right across the street."

"Right—" She stopped. Anything she said now, she'd probably regret. Instead she headed back to the car for the next load, fuming.

So Mitch lived right across the street, did he? He

might have mentioned that little fact about The Willows at some point in their discussion. He hadn't wanted her to come back to Bedford Creek at all; that had been clear. He certainly didn't want her to join in his investigation. But apparently he felt that if she did come, she should be under his eye.

Well, they'd get a few things straight as soon as possible. She was used to doing things on her own, and that wasn't about to change now—

It looked as if she'd have a chance to tell him so in the immediate future, because his police cruiser was pulling up directly across from The Willows.

Mitch got out. He closed the door, hesitated a moment, and then headed straight for her.

"Anne. I see you arrived safely. Any problems?"

"Not at all." She tried for a cool politeness. It would help, she thought, if she didn't experience that jolt of awareness every time she saw his tall figure. "We just got in a few minutes ago."

"I'll take that." He reached for the suitcase she'd begun to pull from the trunk, but she tightened her grip.

"I can handle it."

"I'm sure you can." His hand closed on the bag, his fingers brushing hers. "But why should you?"

"Because I don't need any help." Mitch Donovan had to be the only person in her life with the ability to make her sound like a petulant child.

They stood staring at each other, the bag trapped

between them. Then his lips twitched slightly. "Something tells me that's your favorite saying."

"There's nothing wrong with being independent." She'd had to be, even when she was a child, even when she'd been married. She didn't know any other way to behave.

You can't do it all yourself, child. Helen's voice echoed in her mind. *Sometimes you have to let go and let God help.*

"You can be independent and still let me carry your bag upstairs."

She held on for another moment, then released the handle. With a half smile, he hoisted the bag, then grabbed a second one with his other hand.

Typical cop, she thought, following with an armload of her own. Give him an inch and he'd take a mile.

Unloading the car took only a few minutes with Mitch helping. She glanced around the same sitting room they'd had before, amazed as always at the amount of gear required by one small baby. Mitch set the stroller behind a bentwood coat rack.

"Looks like that's it."

She nodded. Maybe this was the chance she needed to set some ground rules for this visit. He had to understand that she wasn't going to be a passive bystander to any investigation he planned.

"We need to talk. Have you found out anything more about Tina's stay here?"

His eyebrows lifted. "It's only been a day."

"I don't have much time, if you'll recall. The hearing is in less than a month, and the results—"

The sentence came to an abrupt halt when Kate, holding the baby, stuck her head in the door. "Getting settled?"

Anne managed a nod, her heart thumping. In another instant she'd have said something about DNA testing, and Kate would have heard. She'd have to be more careful.

Mitch gestured toward the stroller. "Why don't we take Emilie out for a walk? I'm sure she's tired of being cooped up in the car."

Now that was exactly what she didn't want: to have the whole town see them together and speculate about them. "I don't think so. I need to put things away."

But Kate was already handing the baby to Mitch. "Good idea." She beamed. "This little one could use some fresh air, and the sunshine won't last that much longer. I'll help you put things away later, if you want."

Mitch bounced Emilie, who responded with a delighted squeal. She patted his face with her open palms. He looked at Anne, eyebrows raised, and she knew exactly what he was thinking. If she wanted to talk to him, they might have more privacy on a walk.

With a strong sense of having been outmaneuvered, Anne reached for the stroller.

When they reached the sidewalk in front of the

house, Mitch bent to slide Emilie into her seat. His big hands cradled her, protecting her head as she wiggled. Anne's heart gave an unexpected lurch at the sight. His gentleness dissolved some of the irritation she'd been holding on to, and she tried to retrieve it.

"I understand you live right across the street." *And you should have mentioned that.*

Mitch straightened, nodding. "I bought the house a year ago." He shrugged. "Got tired of living in rented places. I wanted something of my own, where I could decide on the color of the walls and pound a nail in if I wanted to."

The cottage, with its peaked roof and shutters, pristine front door and neatly trimmed hedges, proclaimed its owner's pride.

"It's charming." The house was an unexpected insight into the man. She'd have expected him to live in a furnished apartment, something closer to spartan barracks. "Convenient to the station, too, I guess."

"Just a couple of blocks." He shrugged. "But nothing in Bedford Creek is very far away, as long as you don't mind walking uphill." He smiled. "Or down."

He held the gate open as Anne pushed the stroller through it to the street.

"You might have mentioned this was your neighborhood when you suggested The Willows."

He paused, looking down at her with a quizzical expression. "Does that make a difference?"

"It certainly adds to the impression I'm here to see you." She felt herself blush.

"Believe me, nothing I did or didn't do would change that idea." His hand closed over hers on the stroller handle. "Why don't you let me push?"

She'd put mittens on Emilie, and maybe she should have done the same for herself. If she had, she wouldn't have to feel the warmth and strength of his hand over hers. And Anne wouldn't be struggling with the ripple of that warmth traveling right to her heart.

"Fine." She snatched her hand away. "As long as you push it by the café where Tina worked. I want to see the place for myself."

His answer would tell her whether he was ready to accept her role in finding out the truth about Tina, whatever it was. This would certainly be easier if she didn't have to fight him every step of the way.

But unfortunately, even that wouldn't eliminate the problem that became clearer each time she was with Mitch Donovan. She was ridiculously—and unsuitably—attracted to the man who might be Emilie's father, and who might have the power to take Emilie away.

So Anne wasn't giving up on her determination to play detective, Mitch thought. It would have been too much to hope she might, but somehow he had to convince her. Because if he had a civilian meddling in this situation, he could forget any hope of keeping things quiet while he found out the truth about Tina Mallory and her baby.

"I'll take you to the café." He tried to keep reluctance from showing in his voice. "I'll even buy you a cup of coffee there, if you want."

She glanced up at him as they walked along the street. "Do I sense a 'but' coming?"

He shrugged. "But Cassie Worth, the owner, isn't the most forthcoming person in the world, especially with strangers. I haven't had a chance to sound her out yet. Maybe you'd better let me see what I can find out first."

"Give me a little credit. I didn't intend to cross-examine her."

"Like birds don't intend to fly?"

Her lips twitched in a smile he suspected was involuntary. "Meaning I can't help being an attorney any more than you can help being a cop?"

"Something like that." He eased the stroller over a patch of ice on the sidewalk. He frowned, glancing up at the storefront of Clinton's Candles. Clinton would have to be reminded to keep his walk clear.

"How will I find out anything if I don't ask?"

"If you start asking a lot of questions, it'll get around. Make people curious—more curious than they already are."

They walked in silence for a few minutes, as she apparently considered that.

"I'll be discreet," she said finally. "That's the best I can do."

He glanced at her. Silky hair brushed the collar of her black leather jacket as she moved. There was nothing remotely discreet about the presence of such a beautiful stranger in Bedford Creek, especially one accompanied by a baby. It probably wouldn't do any good to tell her that, but he had to try. Maybe a blunt reminder would get through.

"I have a lot to lose if you're not."

She looked up at him. He seemed to feel her intense blue gaze penetrate the barriers he kept around him.

"I don't see..." She shook her head. "They're your people. Seems to me they'd take your word over a stranger's, if it came to that."

The apple doesn't fall far from the tree. The refrain he'd heard too often in his childhood echoed in his mind, but he wasn't about to share it with Anne. Would anyone, other than Brett and Alex, his closest friends, take his side? He didn't care to put it to the test.

"I thought we agreed neither of us wanted this to become public knowledge."

She glanced at the baby, and her mouth softened. "I don't relish publicity any more than you do. But I have to find out about Tina." She looked back up at him, and he could read the fear in her eyes. "If you're telling me the truth, then I don't have much time."

"I know."

He felt the clock ticking, too. It must be much worse for Anne, with three to four weeks to get back the DNA test results he knew would prove him innocent. And about the same time until her hearing. No wonder she wanted to launch into an investigation.

His steps slowed. "We'll find out. I don't expect you to trust me on this, but I'm telling you the truth. We'll find out."

She nodded, and he thought he saw a sheen of tears in her eyes. "Yes." She cleared her throat. "The café…is it near here?"

"Right across the street." He gestured toward the Bluebird Café. "Let me buy you that cup of coffee."

The baby seemed to enjoy bouncing down over the curb and across the street. She pounded on the stroller tray with both tiny fists.

The Bluebird Café, its façade painted a bright blue to match its name, was one of a series of shops that staggered down either side of Main Street. They were like so many dominoes, looking ready to tumble to the valley floor, but they'd stood where they were for a hundred years or so.

A bit different from Anne's usual setting, he knew, a vision of that luxury high-rise flitting through his mind. What did she think of Bedford Creek in comparison? Of him?

Whoa, back up and erase that. It didn't matter

what Anne thought of him. Not as long as, in the end, she accepted the fact that he wasn't Emilie's father.

Anne held open the frosted glass door, its placard advertising Cassie's chicken-and-dumpling soup. He lifted the stroller up the two steps from the street and pushed it inside, not wasting time looking up for either admiration or approval in those sapphire eyes.

"Not especially crowded," Anne observed, unzipping Emilie's snowsuit.

"Empty, as a matter of fact. It's too late for lunch and too early for supper." He gestured. "So you have your choice of seating."

She picked a booth halfway back, and by the time they were settled, Cassie had appeared from the kitchen.

"Afternoon, Chief." She twitched her bluebird-trimmed apron and shot Anne a suspicious glance. "What can I get you?"

"Coffee?" He raised his eyebrows at Anne, and she nodded. "Two coffees."

"That's it?" Cassie made it sound like a personal affront that they didn't order anything else.

Again he looked at Anne, and she shook her head. "I had lunch on the way." She gave Cassie a hundred-watt smile. "Another time I'll try your chicken-and-dumpling soup."

That smile would have had him picking himself up off the floor, Mitch thought. Cassie just jerked her head in a nod, but her usual grim expression seemed to soften slightly as she plodded back toward the kitchen.

"Does she give all her customers such a warm welcome?"

He leaned against the blue padded seat. "I told you she wouldn't be very forthcoming."

"A clam is more forthcoming." She took an animal cracker from her bag and handed it to Emilie. The baby pounded it once on the stroller tray and then stuffed it into her mouth. "Why did she open a restaurant, of all things, if she didn't want to be around people?"

He shrugged. "Not that many ways to make a living in Bedford Creek. You either work at the furniture factory or you make money off tourists. And Cassie is a good cook. You'd better come back for that chicken-and-dumpling soup."

"I guess I may as well sample the local cuisine while I'm here."

"And chat with her about Tina while you're at it?" That was obviously in her mind. "Maybe you should let me bring the subject up."

She pierced him with an intent look. "Would you, if I didn't push? Or would you ignore it?"

"I said I'd work on it, and I will." He couldn't keep the irritation from his voice. Persistence was a good quality, but he didn't appreciate having it turned on him. "I've already started a couple of lines of inquiry."

She looked as if she'd like to believe him. "What did you find out?"

The *clink* of coffee mugs announced Cassie's return, and Mitch shot Anne a warning glance. Cassie might not be the yakker Wanda was, but he still didn't want her knowing his business.

Cassie slapped down the mugs, more bluebirds fluttering on the white china. She took a step back, then looked at Anne.

"Fresh apple dumplings tomorrow. Get here early if you want it."

He suspected laughter hovered on Anne's lips, but she didn't let it out. "Thanks, I'll remember."

When Cassie was safely back in the kitchen, he shook his head in mock amazement. "Apple dumplings. Believe it or not, you've made an impression. Cassie doesn't offer her apple dumplings to just anyone."

Amusement lit Anne's eyes. "Dumpling soup and apple dumplings? I'd look like a dumpling if I ate like that."

He let his glance take in her slim figure, sleek in dark slacks and a sapphire sweater that matched her eyes. "You don't look as if you need to worry."

She couldn't meet his eyes. "I didn't know investigating was so calorie-intensive."

"Maybe you ought to leave it to the pros. I can tackle the apple dumplings for you."

She shook her head, smiling but stubborn. "What

were you going to tell me before Cassie came back out?''

Right. The message was clear: he'd better keep his mind on business.

''I did some preliminary checking on Tina Mallory. She lived in town for six months, worked for Cassie from June to October. Once the tourist season ended, Cassie let her go. Far as I can tell, she left sometime the following month.''

''Why Philadelphia, I wonder? She never told me that.''

So, he could tell her something she didn't know about her friend. ''Turns out she lived awhile in Philadelphia. I'd guess when she realized she was pregnant, she wanted to go somewhere familiar.''

''Familiar? Do you mean she still had friends or family there?''

Fear probably put the sharp edge in Anne's voice. Maybe it hadn't occurred to her that Tina might have family. Family that could possibly have a claim to Emilie. He shook his head quickly.

''Not that I can tell. Apparently it was always just her and her mother—no father in evidence. And her mother died about four years ago.'' He curled his fingers around the warm mug. ''She'd apparently lost touch with any friends she once had. But there certainly had to be more job opportunities in Philadelphia than anywhere around here.''

''That makes sense. I just wonder why she never

told me she'd lived there. In fact, I'm sure she said she was from Los Angeles."

"Sounds as if Tina was a little careless with the truth at times."

She gave him a level look, one that said she knew just what he meant. "She was young," she said finally. "She tried to make herself interesting. But that doesn't mean I should discount everything she said."

He'd better not let himself enjoy the way Anne's eyes lit up when she smiled, he thought. Or try to figure out a way to prolong moments when they laughed together across the table as if they were friends.

They weren't friends, and Anne obviously intended that they never would be.

Chapter Five

By the next morning, Anne had nearly succeeded in convincing herself she'd imagined that unsuitable attraction to Mitch. It must be a product of emotional stress. She'd ignore the feelings—she'd always been good at that, thanks to her parents' example.

She maneuvered Emilie's stroller over the curb. One thing she knew about parenting without a doubt: Emilie wouldn't grow up in the kind of emotional desert she had. If she and Terry had had children... But she'd finally realized her husband had no desire for a family. In marrying him, she'd just put herself in another emotionally barren situation.

No, not for Emilie. She bent to tuck the snowsuit hood more closely around the baby's ears, since the weather had turned cooler. Emilie would have love overflowing from her mother. If...

The Bluebird Café, she hoped, might provide some answers. At least today she wouldn't have Mitch sitting across from her when she dropped Tina's name into the conversation. If Cassie did know whom Tina had dated, and if that person was Mitch, she might not want to say anything in front of him.

The hardware store carried a display of window boxes and planting tools. Anne hurried past. Not even the most rabid gardener would be buying window boxes today, she thought. But it was easy to imagine the narrow wooden houses, tucked along the steep hillside, decked out with flowers in every window. Bedford Creek would look like a village in the Swiss Alps.

She pulled the café door open, to be greeted by a wave of warm air scented with apples and cinnamon, and accented with chatter. It wasn't noon yet, but the Bluebird was crowded already. It was obviously the place to be when Cassie made her famous apple dumplings.

She glanced around, aware of the flurry of curious looks sent her way. The only empty table, a small one set for two, was in the front window. She maneuvered the stroller to it. Bringing up Tina's name in a casual way wouldn't be easy with the number of people in the café. She would have to linger over her lunch, hoping to outlast most of them.

"Hi. Can I help you?" The waitress was younger

than Cassie, with a name tag showing her name: Heather.

Anne felt a spurt of optimism. This girl, close in age to Tina, might remember more about Tina than Cassie did, assuming she'd worked at the café then.

"I'll have the chicken-and-dumpling soup." She put down the plastic-coated menu and smiled at the girl, whose spiky hair and multiple mismatched earrings had to be a fashion statement in a small town. "I've heard it's your specialty."

"You bet." Heather's hazel eyes ticked off every detail of Anne's slacks, cashmere sweater and gold jewelry. "Cassie's famous for it. Anything for the baby?"

"No, that's it."

She'd wait until the girl came back with her food to build on the conversation. Maybe by then she'd have lost the feeling everyone in the place was listening to her.

She bent to pull a jar of baby peaches from the diaper bag. As she straightened, the door swung open again and Mitch walked in.

Her cheeks were warm because she'd been bending over, that was all. She concentrated on Emilie, aware of Mitch's voice as he exchanged greetings with what sounded like everyone in the place. With any luck, he'd be joining one of them for lunch.

Apparently luck didn't have anything to do with it. Mitch made his way, unhurriedly, to her table.

The chair scraped, and he sat down across from her as if they'd had a lunch date.

"Somehow I thought I'd find you here." He bent to greet Emilie, who responded with a crow of delight when he tickled her.

"Probably because I mentioned yesterday I wanted to come back for the chicken-dumpling soup." *And a private conversation with Cassie.*

His smile told her he knew exactly what she was thinking. "Good day for it." He waved across the room to Heather. "Another bowl of the chicken soup here, Heather."

The girl nodded. "You bet, Chief."

"You guessed—" At his warning glance she lowered her voice. "You guessed I wanted to talk with Cassie myself. I'd rather do it in private."

"You mean without me around." His face kept its relaxed expression, probably for the benefit of anyone who might be watching, but his eyes turned to stone. "I have an interest in this, remember?"

"I remember." She could so easily see his side of it. If he was innocent, naturally he'd want to protect himself by knowing anything she found out. Unfortunately, if he was guilty, the same thing applied.

"Then you can understand why I'm here." His square jaw seemed carved from granite.

"All right." She didn't have much choice. She needed his cooperation, whether she liked it or not. "Let me bring it up."

"Go ahead. But don't be surprised if she can't

tell you much. If you haven't been here during tourist season, you can't imagine how crazy it is.''

The soup arrived in huge, steaming pottery bowls. Heather put down a basket of freshly baked rolls nestled in a blue-checked napkin. She looked from Anne to Mitch.

"Anything else I can get you? Chief, don't you want a sandwich with that? Cassie made pulled pork barbecue.''

"I'm saving room for a dumpling. You've got one back there with my name on it, haven't you?"

"Sure thing." Heather smiled, touching one earring with a plum-colored nail.

Anne could so easily imagine Mitch having this conversation with Tina. Could imagine this sort of encounter, day after day, leading to an invitation, then to an involvement he might later regret.

"Sounds as if you've been waiting on the chief for a long time.'' That probably wasn't the most tactful way into what she wanted to ask, but she couldn't think of a better one.

Heather shrugged. "Almost a year I've been working here. You get to know the regulars, believe me." The girl frowned at the sound of a persistent bell from the kitchen, then spun away, bluebird-trimmed apron rustling.

"I could have told you Heather didn't work here when Tina did.''

"I'd rather find out for myself.''

He shrugged. "I figured." He dipped the spoon into his soup.

"Attorneys prefer to ask the questions." She took a spoonful, and rich chicken flavor exploded in her mouth, chasing away the chill. "It's in my blood, I'm afraid."

"A whole family of lawyers?" He sounded as if that were the worst fate he could imagine.

"Just my father. He has a corporate practice in Hartford."

"Your mother's not a lawyer, too?"

She tried to imagine her mother doing anything so mundane, and failed. "My mother's social life keeps her occupied. And I don't have any brothers or sisters." The last thing she wanted to discuss right now was her parents. Their reaction to Emilie had been predictable, but it had still hurt. "What about you? Big family?"

She'd thought the expression in his eyes chilly before; now it had frozen. "One brother. My mother died when I was in high school. My father was long gone by then."

"I'm sorry." She suspected pain moved behind the mask he wore, but he'd never show it, not to her, probably not to anyone. "That must have made you and your brother very close."

He shrugged. "Link works heavy construction, mostly out west. He hasn't been back to Bedford Creek in a couple of years."

Anne's heart constricted. Loneliness. She recognized the symptoms. He probably wouldn't believe her if she said she knew how he felt. He probably wouldn't believe having wealthy parents who'd stayed married to each other didn't guarantee a happy family life. Didn't guarantee you wouldn't marry someone just like them. She felt the familiar regret that her marriage hadn't been…more, somehow. Deeper.

By the time their apple dumplings arrived, most of the crowd had filtered out of the café. Anne took one look at the immense dumpling, served in its own small iron skillet, and swallowed hard.

Her face must have given her away, because Mitch chuckled. "Somebody should have warned you, I guess. But you have to make a stab at it, because Cassie will be out to see how you like it."

"That's more dessert than I eat in a month."

Mitch plunged his fork into flaky pastry, and apple syrup spurted out, mixing with the mound of whipped cream. "Live dangerously. It's worth it."

The first taste melted in her mouth. By the time Cassie appeared, ready to accept applause, Anne had made a respectable dent in the dumpling.

"Wonderful, absolutely wonderful." She leaned back in her chair. "I couldn't eat another bite."

Cassie's thin lips creased in what might have been a smile. "I'll wrap it up for you. You can finish it later."

There was nothing to do but smile and nod. "I'll do that. It was just as good as I'd heard it was."

Cassie smoothed her apron. "You hear that from Mitch?"

"It might have been Mitch who told me. Or it might have been a friend of mine who used to work here. Maybe you remember her. Tina Mallory?"

Cassie frowned. "Little bit of a thing? Big blue eyes?"

"Yes, that's Tina." She held her breath. Was she about to find out something?

"Let's see...it wasn't this past season. One before, I guess. Good waitress. What's she up to now?"

"I'm afraid she passed away a few months ago."

"A kid like that?" Cassie shook her head. "You just never know, do you? I'm sorry to hear it."

"I'd hoped to meet her friends while I'm here in Bedford Creek. Do you know of anyone she was especially close to...a boyfriend, maybe?"

The woman sniffed. "Got enough to do without keeping track of the summer help's boyfriends, believe me. Can't recall anybody offhand. She came in, did her job, got along with the customers. None of my business who she hung out with after work."

Anne's hope shriveled with each word. It looked as if this would be a dead end, like so much about Tina. "If you think of anyone, would you let me know?"

"If I do."

Cassie's tone said she doubted it. Apparently Tina

had passed through Cassie's life without leaving a trace.

She picked up the dumpling pans. "I'll put this in a box for you."

When she'd gone, Anne met Mitch's gaze. His look was unexpectedly sympathetic.

"Sorry. I know you hoped she'd remember something."

"It's a small town. I thought everyone knew everything in a small town."

"They do, believe me." There was an edge to Mitch's words. "But that's only regarding the other locals. When the town is flooded with tourists and summer help, you might not notice your best friend on the street."

She still found that hard to picture, but apparently it was true. If so, the chances of finding anyone who remembered anything about Tina had diminished.

"You think I ought to give up." That was what he had in mind; she was sure of it.

He shrugged. "I think you ought to leave it to me. But I suspect you're not going to."

"If you—" She stopped, realizing Cassie had emerged from the kitchen with the leftover dumpling.

"There you go." Cassie deposited the package in front of her, patting it as if it were a pet. "And I thought of something. About that friend of yours."

Anne struggled to keep the eagerness from her

voice. "Did you remember someone who knew her?"

"In a manner of speaking. Seems to me she roomed with another one of the summer waitresses—girl named Marcy Brown."

"Is she here?"

Cassie shook her head almost before the words were out of her mouth. "Summer help, that's all she was. Went off at the end of the season. None of those girls stick around once the season's over. No jobs for them."

Anne tried to swallow her disappointment. "Do you know where she went from here?"

"Seems to me she was headed someplace warm for the winter. Key West, I think it was." Cassie's expression showed disapproval. "Those kids...they just flit from place to place. I might have an address for her, if I had to send her last check, but she's probably long gone by now."

"I'd like to have it just the same, if you can find it."

The woman nodded. "See what I can do, when I have the time." She frowned. "There was one other thing."

"What's that?"

"Seems to me both those girls got into that singles group Pastor Richie had at Grace Church. Maybe someone there kept up with her."

"Thank you." She was past worrying about what Cassie thought of her interest. "I appreciate it."

It was something. Not much, but a little something that just might lead somewhere.

And as for the frown in Mitch's brown eyes... well, it wasn't unexpected, was it. She'd just have to live with his disapproval, because it probably wouldn't change.

So, it looked as if he'd been wrong about how helpful Cassie might be. But then, Mitch had been wrong about a lot of things since the moment Anne walked into his life.

Those blue eyes of hers were intent on her prize. This lead to Tina's friend would encourage her. If he didn't get control of her search, she'd be chasing it all over Bedford Creek. And sooner or later someone would find out why.

"I suppose you want to rush off to Pastor Richie right now."

"Maybe not this precise moment. But it is a lead to Tina's roommate."

"That was eighteen months ago. The chance that Pastor Richie knows where to find this Marcy Brown isn't very great."

"I have to try."

A stubborn look firmed her mouth, and he suppressed the urge to smooth it away with his finger. That would really be counterproductive.

"Look, I know Simon Richie. Why don't you let me talk to him?"

"How do you know him?"

She'd probably think this coincidence suspicious, but it couldn't be helped. "Because I go to Grace Church."

Her eyebrows lifted. "Did you also belong to the singles group?"

"No." People went to that, for the most part, because they wanted a social life. He didn't, so he didn't attend. "But I know Simon Richie pretty well. The questions would come better from me."

"I'd rather ask him myself."

Somehow this sounded familiar. If Anne Morden ever depended on anybody but herself, he had yet to see it.

"Look, if you go walking into Simon's office asking about this girl, it's going to make people wonder."

"I don't see why. I'll just say I'm a friend of a friend."

She clearly still didn't see the rampant curiosity with which people in town surveyed her every move.

"Let me find a less obvious way of going about it."

She seemed to be weighing that, and for a moment he thought she'd agree.

"Grace Church...isn't that where Kate belongs?"
He nodded.

"Kate's invited me to go to a church potluck supper with her tonight. I'm sure I'll have a chance to meet your Pastor Richie. I can bring up the subject casually.''

He pictured her mentioning it in front of several of the most notorious gossips in town. She was determined, so there was only one thing he could do.

''Fine.'' He smiled. ''I'll pick you up at ten to six, then.''

Her eyes narrowed. ''What do you mean?''

''Didn't Kate tell you? We often go to the church suppers together.'' *Sometimes, anyway.*

He was doing what he had to. If he expected to stay in control of this situation, he needed to keep tabs on Anne.

Unfortunately, he had a strong suspicion he had another motivation.

''Well, don't you look nice.'' Kate turned from the kitchen stove to assess Anne and Emilie. ''Both of you.''

Anne brushed one hand down the soft wool of her emerald skirt. It matched the green of Emilie's jumper, so she'd decided to wear it. ''Is it too dressy?''

Kate shook her head. ''You look as pretty as a picture. I'm sure Mitch will say the same.''

Oh, dear. There it was again: Kate's insistence on pairing the two of them up like bookends.

When she'd returned to the house earlier and told Kate they were going to the potluck, the elderly woman had been delighted. Anne had tried to dissuade Kate's all-too-obvious matchmaking, to no avail.

Well, what should she say? That Mitch wouldn't care how she looked? That the only reason he'd decided to take them to the potluck was to keep her from blurting out something indiscreet to Pastor Richie? It was only too obvious that that was behind his sudden desire to go with them.

There wasn't a thing she could do about Kate's misapprehension, so she might just as well change the subject. "Are you sure I can't fix something? Or stop at the bakery and buy a cake?"

"Goodness, no. There'll be more food than we can eat in a week, as it is. Everyone brings way too much stuff to these suppers."

Anne had to smile. Kate's righteous assertion was undercut by the fact that she'd prepared an enormous chicken-and-broccoli casserole, and even now was putting a pumpkin pie into her picnic basket.

"You don't think you're taking quite a bit yourself?"

"This little thing? Why, Mitch will probably eat half my casserole himself. That boy does love home cooking…probably because his mother never had time to cook much for them." Kate's eyes were filled with sympathy. "You do know about Mitch's family, don't you?"

"I know his mother died when he was in high school." She held Emilie a little closer.

"Well, his father had left before that. Poor

woman worked to take care of those two boys. I'm sure no one could blame her if she wasn't there to cook supper every night. Or if she went out now and then, just to cheer herself up.'' Kate yanked open a drawer, muttering to herself about potholders.

Reading between the lines, it sounded as if Mitch had pretty much raised himself. Probably that, along with the military, had made him the person he was.

And what kind of person was that? Anne stared out the window above the sink, where dusk had begun to close in on Kate's terraced hillside garden. A man who'd buried his emotions—that's what she'd thought the first time she'd seen him, and nothing had changed her mind about that. A man who had to be in control, whatever the situation.

That might make him a good cop. But it wasn't a quality, given her strong independent streak, that she'd ever found appealing in a man. Besides, she wasn't interested. In future, her family would consist of Emilie and her, that was all.

She'd told herself she could ignore the attraction she felt for Mitch. Unfortunately, it didn't seem to be working. That attraction kept popping to the surface every time they were together.

Well, if she couldn't ignore it, she could at least control it. She'd remind herself twenty times a day, if she had to, that he wasn't the kind of man for her, even without the complication of Emilie's parentage.

The doorbell rang. Kate, her hands full of casserole, nodded toward the front hallway. "Would you mind getting that, dear? It'll be Mitch, I'm sure."

"Of course." Carrying Emilie, she walked down the hall. This was a good chance to test her resolution. She swung open the door.

"Come in, please. Kate's almost ready."

Mitch stepped into the hallway, seeming to fill it. "Hey, there, Miss Emilie, are you ready to go to church?"

Emilie bounced and held out her arms to him.

"Let me take her."

Anne started to turn away just as he reached for the baby, and his hands clasped her arms instead. For a moment they stood touching, the baby between them.

Mitch's large hands tightened, their warmth penetrating the soft wool of her sweater. They were so close that she could see the network of lines at the corners of his eyes, the sweep of his dark lashes, a tiny scar at the corner of his mouth. Those chocolate eyes fixed on hers, and she could hear his breathing quicken. She had to fight the urge to step forward, right into his arms.

She took a deep breath, released Emilie to him, and stepped back. "I'll just get our coats." Astonishing, that her voice could sound so calm.

Obviously reminding herself twenty times a day wasn't going to be enough.

Chapter Six

It was a good thing Anne had pulled away when she did, Mitch decided as he drove them to the church. A very good thing. Because if she hadn't, he just might have kissed her.

Disaster—that's what it would have been, plain and simple. The woman already suspected him of seducing a young girl and leaving her pregnant. What would she think of him if he tried to kiss her?

He pulled into the church parking lot and found a space. He'd better get his head on straight where Anne was concerned. The best way to deal with his inappropriate feelings was to solve Anne's problem for her so she could leave, as soon as possible. And the next step in doing that was to get the information from Pastor Richie himself, and do it without arousing anyone's suspicions.

"Looks like a good turnout." He held open the door to the church's fellowship hall.

"Goodness, half the town must be here." Kate bustled in, depositing her picnic basket on the nearest table. "Now, Mitch, why don't you get one of the high chairs for Emilie before they're all gone. I'll find us a nice place and introduce Anne around."

A warning bell went off in his brain as he went reluctantly in search of a high chair. Who did Kate have in mind for Anne to meet? He could think of at least a half-dozen gossips of both sexes he'd just as soon she avoided.

He'd have to keep an eye on her while looking for a chance to talk to Simon Richie before she did. Right at this moment, he could use a little help.

And there it was. With a sense of relief, he spotted Alex Caine's tall, lean figure. Alex, like Brett, was a friend he could count on. He'd help keep Anne out of trouble.

He deposited the high chair, muttered an excuse to Anne, who seemed to be avoiding his eyes, and worked his way through the crowd to Alex.

"Alex. I'm glad to see you."

His friend, leaning on the stick he sometimes used since surviving a plane crash a year ago, gave him a sardonic look. "Don't you mean you're surprised to see me?"

He grinned. "That, too." Another legacy of the accident seemed to be that Alex didn't socialize much.

"I decided this was my best chance to see your Ms. Morden. And baby."

"Not my Ms. Morden." *And not my baby.* But he didn't need to say that to Alex. He'd said it once, and it was a measure of their friendship that Alex accepted his denial without question.

Alex's gaze rested on Anne. "Kate seems to have adopted her already. Are you sure it was a good idea to bring her and the baby here?"

"Kate invited them. And once Anne found out Simon Richie might have some information on the girl's roommate, there was no stopping her from coming."

Alex took a step or two toward the wall, so they were safely out of the flow of traffic and of earshot. "Have you remembered anything else about the girl—Tina, was it?"

"Tina." He gave a frustrated shake of his head. "What's to remember? I barely knew her. She was a nice kid who poured my morning coffee, that's it. I can't figure why she'd lie about something like this."

"I'd hate to believe you're never going to know the reason."

He could see Alex's mind ticking over possibilities. Even back in high school, Alex had always been the one with the analytical approach to everything. Where Brett had relied on charm and Mitch on strength, Alex had been the thinker of the team.

"The roommate's the best bet, I suppose," Alex

said. "If anyone knows who the girl dated, she would."

Mitch frowned, watching Anne settle Emilie in the high chair. "It just keeps eating at me. Why me? Why did she give my name?"

Alex was silent for a long moment, so long that Mitch turned to look at him. He encountered a searching gaze. "Have you thought about Link?"

Mitch's stomach twisted at the name. *Link.* His brother. "Yes." He bit off the word. "Of course I have. I know what you're thinking. Using my name would be just the sort of sick joke he'd find funny. But you're forgetting, the girl knew me. Besides, he wasn't in Bedford Creek then."

"You sure?"

"I'm sure." Link had a tendency to show up on Mitch's doorstep whenever he was broke or in trouble. "We had a fight the last time he was here, that previous spring. A bad one. I told him I was done bailing him out. He hasn't been back since." He managed a half smile. "I'd like to believe that means he's gotten his act together, but I doubt it."

"People change."

"Not Link." *Not our father.*

Alex shrugged. "I'll take your word for it. Look, they're starting to get the food ready. You need my help with something before I round up my son for dinner?"

"Just keep an eye on Anne. I want to see Simon alone before she has a chance to collar him. But I don't want her getting the third degree from any of our local busybodies.''

"And you expect me to prevent that?" Alex lifted an eyebrow. "You're underestimating them."

"But I'm not overestimating you." Mitch grinned. "You know they're intimidated by the Caine name. And you can flatten anybody with that superior look of yours. Just use it."

Simon Richie charged into the hall then, filled with an energy that never ceased to amaze Mitch. Simon had to be close to sixty, but nothing slowed him down when it came to taking care of his flock. If either Tina or her roommate had left an address, Simon would find it.

"I'm going to try and catch him after he says the blessing," Mitch said. "Remember, keep your eye on Anne."

Alex sketched him a mock salute. "Will do."

He bowed his head and tried to concentrate on the words of the prayer. Simon had an informal way of addressing God that made Him sound like a personal friend Simon was inviting to share their meal. It always made him vaguely uncomfortable. Mitch believed, of course. But Simon seemed to have found a closeness that had always eluded Mitch.

The prayer over, a wave of people swept toward the long serving table. Anne still stood at her chair, eyes closed in prayer for another moment. The sight seemed to clutch his heart. What prayer kept her so still, so focused?

* * *

Anne gripped the plate Kate had given her and edged closer to the serving table. Kate had insisted on watching Emilie so she could go first, since Mitch seemed to have disappeared. She'd noticed him talking to a man Kate said was Alex Caine, owner of Bedford Creek's only industry. The next time she looked, he was gone.

Not that she cared. The memory of that moment in Kate's front hall made her uncomfortable. She hadn't come to this dinner to be with Mitch.

"I don't think we've met." The woman in front of her smiled a welcome. "Let me introduce you to some of these hungry people."

By the time she'd reached the end of the buffet table, half-a-dozen names buzzed in her mind and way too much food had found its way onto her plate. She'd begun to feel that all she'd done since arriving in Bedford Creek was eat.

"I'm finished." She deposited her plate across from Kate, next to the high chair Mitch had put at the end of the table. "You go on now, Kate."

Kate rose and looked around the crowded room with a frown. "I don't know where Mitch is. He'd better get back here before the food's gone."

"I don't think there's any danger of that." And she'd probably have a more placid meal if he weren't sitting next to her, drawing her awareness with every breath.

She'd just given Emilie a biscuit to chew on when

she became conscious of someone standing across from her. She looked up to meet an intent stare.

The older woman's narrow face formed a brief smile. "You'll be Kate's new guest."

Anne nodded. "Anne Morden. This is Emilie."

"I'm Enid Lawrence." The woman's gaze swerved, sharply curious, to the baby and back again. "Tell me, what brings you to Bedford Creek?"

Anne should have been better prepared for a direct question, she thought. As she groped for an answer, someone intervened.

"Excuse me, Enid." It was the man she'd seen Mitch talking with earlier. "I think your daughter is trying to get your attention." He diverted the woman smoothly away from the table, taking the chair she'd been blocking. "I'll keep Anne company until Kate gets back."

Enid Lawrence frowned. For a moment Anne thought she'd argue, but then she nodded, giving Anne a frosted look. "We'll talk later." It almost sounded like a threat.

She moved away, and Anne assessed Mitch's friend, Alex Caine. He was tall, nearly as tall as Mitch, but not as broadly built. His lean, aristocratic face was handsome, but marred by a scar that ran along one cheek. He had the inward look Anne had seen before in people who lived with pain.

"Alex Caine." He held out his hand. "Sorry if I

interrupted, but Enid can be overwhelming at times. 'Curiosity' is her middle name.''

She lifted her eyebrows. ''Did Mitch suggest I needed protecting?''

She caught a flash of surprise mixed with amusement in his dark eyes. ''You caught us, I'm afraid. Mitch thought you might prefer not to explain why you're here too many times tonight.''

Now it was her turn to be surprised. ''Mitch told you?'' She'd have expected him to guard that information more carefully.

''Mitch and I go back a long way. He doesn't keep many secrets from me. Or from Brett.''

''I see.''

He frowned. ''I'm not sure you do. I know Mitch as well as I know anyone. He tells me he didn't—'' He stopped, probably reminded of the number of people in the room. ''Let's just say I'd trust him with my life.'' Some emotion she couldn't identify flickered in his eyes. ''In fact, I already have.''

A dozen questions bubbled to her tongue, but she didn't have a chance to ask any of them. Kate came back, and in the flurry as she settled, Alex excused himself. The next instant, someone slid into the chair next to her. She didn't need to look to know it was Mitch. That aura of solid strength touched her senses.

He brushed her sleeve. She looked, startled, to find he was handing her a slip of paper.

"What's this?" She started to unfold it, but his hand closed over hers.

"It's that information you wanted—"

His fingers tightened a little, and her skin seemed to tingle from their pressure.

"—the latest address and phone number Pastor Richie could find. I had him jot it down for you."

She looked at the address, somewhere in Florida, written in an unfamiliar hand on church stationery. She folded the paper and slipped it in her bag.

"I didn't expect you to do that. Thank you."

"My pleasure." A smile tugged at his mouth. "No ulterior motives, I promise you. I just thought it would cause less comment if I asked. I hope you find her."

Perhaps he didn't expect her to believe that, but it sounded genuine. He'd given the information to her, rather than following up on it himself. Almost as if they could trust each other.

Careful, her lawyer's mind cautioned. *Look at all the evidence, then make a decision.*

She'd like, just this once, to rely on her instinct, the instinct that said he was telling the truth. That he could be trusted.

Unfortunately she couldn't. Not with Emilie's future at stake.

Anne rolled the stroller through the police station doorway, the memory of the last time she'd done that flickering through her mind. Only a few days ago, but it seemed like a lifetime. Odd, that she'd begun to feel at home in Bedford Creek so quickly, almost as if it had been waiting for her.

"Ms. Morden!" Wanda exclaimed. "Look who's here, Chief."

Mitch stood in the doorway to his office, ushering someone inside. He swung around at Wanda's words. Anne wasn't mistaking the warmth in his eyes at the sight of her, was she?

"Anne. I hoped I'd see you today." He sent a glance toward his office. "Trouble is, I have someone here right now. Can you wait?"

Aware of Wanda's sharp eyes dissecting every gesture, Anne nodded. "Actually, I have a couple of errands to run. Why don't I come back in, say, half an hour."

"Sounds good." He reached past her to hold the door for the stroller, and his hand brushed her shoulder. "I'll see you then."

She pushed the stroller up the sidewalk, still feeling that casual touch. When the number Pastor Richie had passed on proved no longer valid, directory assistance and even the pastor had been unable to help her further. She had no choice but to ask Mitch for his help in tracking down Marcy Brown. But now she wondered if she'd made the right decision in bringing this to him. Everything Mitch had done was consistent with his being an honorable man who was telling her the truth. But could she rely on him to trace Tina's roommate?

The street staggered its way up the hill, and by the time she reached the pharmacy she was winded. She purchased shampoo and a teething ring, then glanced at her watch as she went out the door. Another fifteen minutes before Mitch expected her.

Someone had placed a bright yellow bench outside the pharmacy, probably for the convenience of all those tourists everyone assured her showed up in the summer. She sat down, positioning the stroller so the baby was out of the wind. The weak sunshine touched her cheeks, a promise of summer to come. A fat robin, back from his trip south, perched on the edge of a sidewalk planter and cocked his head.

A shadow fell across her. "Ms. Morden."

She looked up at the woman who'd introduced herself at the church supper the night before—the woman Alex had seemed determined to help her avoid. Her mind scrambled briefly, then came up with a name.

"Mrs. Lawrence. It's nice to see you again." Or was it? Alex had steered the woman off, implying she was a gossip, and that avid look in her eyes seemed to confirm it.

"I hoped I'd run into you." The woman perched on the bench next to her, tucking her brown wool coat around her legs. "We didn't have a chance to get acquainted last night. I'm Enid."

"I met so many people last night. Your congregation is so friendly to a stranger. It made me feel at home."

"You're from Philadelphia." The woman made it a statement, as if docketing facts. "Kate told me that. But she didn't say why you're here."

Anne edged an inch farther from that blatant curiosity. "Didn't she?"

Enid Lawrence shook her head with an affronted look, as if she had a right to every morsel of knowledge she could collect. "She didn't. It's not to see Chief Donovan, I hope?"

Anne weighed the probable results of outright rudeness in deterring the woman and decided even that wouldn't work. "Not exactly," she evaded. "Bedford Creek is so charming. I understand you have quite a lot of visitors."

"Tourists." She sniffed. "But I'm glad you're not here to see that Mitch Donovan."

The venom in the woman's voice startled her. Everyone she'd met thus far seemed devoted to Mitch. Enid Lawrence seemed to be the exception.

Enid apparently took silence for interest. "He's not really one of us, you know."

"One of us?" She'd certainly had the impression Mitch had grown up in Bedford Creek. What was the woman driving at?

"He's a Donovan." Enid sniffed again. "Everyone in town knows what the Donovans are like. Worthless, the lot of them. The father would steal anything that wasn't nailed down, and those boys were just as bad. Carousing, getting into one scrape after another. Troublemakers, both of them. As for the mother and her drinking…''

The venom had spilled out so quickly that Anne hadn't had time to react. Suddenly revulsion ripped through her with an almost physical shudder. She got up quickly. ''I'm afraid I have to go.''

Enid frowned. ''I'm just telling you because you're a newcomer. I wouldn't want you to be taken in.''

''I don't care to discuss Chief Donovan with you.'' Her anger surprised her. Shouldn't she be taking the opportunity to find out anything she could about Mitch? Instead, she felt the need to defend him.

The woman rose, bringing her eyes to a level with Anne's. ''Fine, if that's all the thanks I get for taking an interest. Mitch Donovan wouldn't even be here if Alex Caine didn't owe him something.''

Anne managed to get the stroller out from beside the bench, her hands shaking a little. ''Excuse me, please.''

She swung the stroller around and set off downhill, heels clicking in her rush to get away from the woman. No wonder Alex Caine had intervened last night. The woman was absolutely poisonous.

Her words trickled through Anne's mind. Mitch was not trustworthy—that was the gist of it. The woman was convinced Mitch was no good, apparently because of his father's reputation.

Unfair, her instincts shouted. That was unfair. The

woman had no right blackening Mitch's reputation because of what his father had done.

But she'd also talked about trouble Mitch and his brother had gotten into, had implied that made him not trustworthy. Trusting him was what she was about to do. And it was something she didn't do easily.

Her impetuous charge down the hill had already brought her to the police station. If she saw Mitch while Enid Lawrence's bitter words echoed in her ears... Fair or not, she just couldn't do it. She'd have to go back to the house and think this over.

"Anne." Mitch opened the door and held it for her. "I've been watching for you. Come in."

She could feel herself flushing. "It was nothing important. I don't need to bother you now."

His brown eyes seemed to frost over. He stepped onto the walk and closed the door. "Don't you mean you've just had an interesting discussion with Enid Lawrence?"

She felt as guilty as if she'd sought out the woman. "How did you know she was talking to me?"

He jerked his head toward the bench outside the pharmacy. "I was watching for you to come back. I saw your little chat."

"I certainly didn't instigate it."

"You didn't avoid it, either." His jaw looked tight.

Her faint feelings of guilt changed to anger. "I

walked away from her, in case you didn't notice. I'm not interested in gossip, even if—''

"Even if it supports the things you'd like to believe about me?"

His expression froze as a passerby eyed them. She seized a chance to gain control.

"I didn't go looking for the woman." She lowered her voice. "I'm not soliciting gossip about you, if that's what you think."

That probably was exactly how it looked, and there wasn't a thing she could do about it.

Or maybe there was.

The words pressed on her lips, wanted to be said. She could take the woman seriously or not. If she didn't, there was an easy way to prove it, by asking for his help.

She took a deep breath. "Now can we forget Enid Lawrence?" She wasn't sure she could, but she wanted to try. "I need your help. I want you to help me find Marcy Brown."

A few minutes later they walked back toward the house together, in tacit agreement that the subject was better discussed away from the station.

Anne looked carefully at her feelings. Could she forget Enid's poisoned words?

"Worried about it?"

She glanced up at Mitch, startled and guilty, then realized he was talking about the roommate, not about what Enid had said.

"No, not worried, exactly." She could hardly tell

him she was trying to sort out her opinion of him. "Concerned about the time element, I suppose. How will you try to find Marcy?"

"Plenty of ways to track people down." He frowned. "The trouble is, this isn't a police case. It limits what I can do."

That hadn't occurred to her. "What *can* you do?" She hoped her question didn't sound as sharp to him as it did to her. If he couldn't or wouldn't use police resources, what good had it done to ask him?

"Believe me, if people knew how easy it is to get information on them, they'd be shocked. I can follow up on her social security number and credit reports, for a start."

"That should lead somewhere, surely. It's not as if the woman is trying to hide from us. She doesn't know we're looking for her."

"We'll find her." He slowed while she eased the stroller over a bump in the walk. "I just hope she knows something useful."

"Girlfriends do talk to each other."

He nodded. "That's about what Alex said. He thinks Tina had to have confided in someone, and who better than her roommate."

"I hope we're both right." She stuffed her hands in her jacket pockets. "He surprised me last night. When I realized you'd told him, I mean."

"We don't keep many secrets from each other."

It was much the same thing Alex had said. "He told me he'd trusted you with his life." She hadn't intended to say that, and knew it sounded like prying.

"Ancient history."

Enid had implied Alex's friendship was somehow owed to Mitch, and the thought left an acrid taste in her mouth. She didn't want to think that about either of them. She wanted to believe they were who they seemed to be.

"Is it something you can talk about?"

His gaze rested on her face for a long moment, then he shrugged. "If you want to hear it. It's not a big secret. Just some trouble we got into when—"

He stopped abruptly, then swung away from her. "Just a second."

Before she could say a word, he'd vaulted over the picket fence in front of the house they were passing. He plunged into the shrubbery by the porch and emerged a second later with a wriggling captive. Davey Flagler.

Apparently Mitch's police instincts never shut off. That was something important to remember as she tried to understand him. He was always a cop.

Chapter Seven

❧

Great. As if things weren't already bad enough, now Davey had to act up again. Mitch tightened his grip on the boy, who wiggled like a fish on a hook.

He couldn't kid himself. Anne's opinion of him had probably taken a nosedive after her little chat with Enid Lawrence, and no wonder. He could just imagine what Enid had to say about him and his family.

Davey was going to make matters worse. Anne would go into her defense attorney mode; she wouldn't be able to stop herself. And they'd be adversaries again, armed with their own visions of what was right.

Well, it couldn't be helped. He had a job to do, and he was going to do it, regardless of what Anne thought of him.

"Trespassing, Davey?" He eyed the culprit. "You wouldn't have been thinking about that package on Mrs. Jefferson's porch, now would you?"

"I don't know what you're talking about." Sullen black eyes stared up at him. "You're crazy."

Over the boy's head he caught the flicker of surprise that crossed Anne's face. She hadn't noticed the package, any more than she'd noticed the kid. Being a cop had heightened his ability to register what other people didn't.

"Crazy?" He glared at Davey. "I'd be crazy to take your word for anything. Go ahead, tell me what you were doing in Mrs. Jefferson's yard."

"I wasn't after any package." Davey nearly spat the words at him. "I thought I heard a cat."

He could almost see the wheels turning in Davey's brain as he tried to come up with a plausible story. At least the kid wasn't an accomplished liar—yet.

"It looked like it was hurt." Davey put on a righteous expression that wouldn't have convinced the most gullible person in the world. "I was just trying to help. You always think I'm doing something wrong."

"That's because you usually are." Anger surged, and he shoved it down. A cop had no right to feel anger. That wasn't part of his job. Mitch didn't know why Davey set off a firestorm within him every time he dealt with the kid, but he had to stay detached.

"The boy didn't actually take anything, as far as I can tell."

Anne's intervention didn't do a thing to douse his anger. "Only because I grabbed him first," he said, tightening his grip as Davey wiggled again. "Guess I'll have to speak to the delivery man about leaving things on porches. Looks like that's just too much temptation."

"You're declaring him guilty without any evidence at all." Anne's eyes shot angry sparks. "You don't know what was in his mind."

"Just stay out of it, Counselor. I don't need advice on how to do my job."

"Maybe you do. You can't accuse someone of something that hasn't been done yet."

"Look, this isn't the big city." Anne would never understand what things were like in a small town. Or why.

"Believe me, I'm only too aware of that. You wouldn't get away with this there—not without someone filing a complaint, anyway."

He counted to ten. It didn't help. "A cop in a small town is different. People expect us to anticipate trouble, and most times we can. And they expect us to prevent it, not wait around until it happens."

He had a sudden mental image of himself explaining, talking too much in front of the kid, and knew it was because he wanted Anne to think well of him. And that was probably an impossible goal.

"You can't—" she began.

"Yes, I can."

He turned to the still squirming boy. He had to concentrate on his job, not on what Anne thought of him.

"I want to see you and your father at the station tomorrow, right after school."

"But my dad might have to work. Or maybe—"

"No excuses, just be there. Because if you're not, I'll come after you. Got it?"

Davey's mouth set, and he nodded.

Mitch released his grip. Davey didn't bother trying to act macho. He just ran.

Mitch watched him go, then turned back to Anne, knowing he'd see condemnation in her eyes.

"I suppose you're proud of yourself, bullying a boy like that."

"What do you know about 'a boy like that'?" His anger flared again, startling him.

"I know anyone would respond better to kindness than to threats."

"Kindness!" She didn't understand. She never would. "Let me tell you what it's going to take for Davey Flagler to turn into a decent citizen instead of winding up in big trouble. He's going to have to work harder, perform better, be smarter than anyone else, because he's starting a lot of steps behind. And he won't do that if people make excuses for him."

Anne looked at him for a long moment, blue eyes

blazing in a white face. "Are you talking about Davey Flagler? Or are you talking about yourself?"

She didn't wait for an answer. She walked away quickly, head high, pushing the stroller toward Kate's place and leaving Mitch fuming.

Hours later Anne slowed as she approached the front porch of Mitch's house. She stopped just beyond the pool of light from the street lamp. When she'd told Kate she needed to talk to Mitch, Kate had been only too eager to watch Emilie for her.

The windows of his small house glowed with a warm yellow light. She shivered, huddling a little deeper into her jacket. The temperature had dropped like a stone the moment the sun went down, and the stars were crystalline in a black sky.

She couldn't stand out here in the dark and the cold. She might as well march right up to the door and get this over with.

Her cheeks went hot in spite of the cold air. She couldn't believe she'd spoken to Mitch the way she had. Even if she had been right, they didn't have the kind of relationship that allowed her to say something so personal.

Lord, I'm sorry. I let my temper get the better of me again. I acted as if I knew what was right for everyone.

Confessing her mistake was one step in the right direction. Now she had to tell Mitch. She bit her lip. She had to tell him, because that was the right thing to do. It was also the only way to get things back on an even keel between them. That was all she wanted.

She went quickly up the steps and rang the bell.

Mitch opened the door, a dark bulk against the light behind him in the hallway. She couldn't make out his expression, which might be just as well.

"Anne. I'm surprised to see you."

He said the words in such a neutral tone that she didn't know what to make of his mood. "I came over to apologize." It was better just to blurt it out. "I said things I shouldn't have this afternoon, and I wouldn't want you to…"

The sentence died out. The problem was that she really did think she knew why he reacted to Davey as he did. She just didn't have the right to say so.

"Forget it." He stepped back, opening the door wider. "Come in. You don't have to stand out there in the cold."

"I shouldn't. I left Emilie with Kate, and I wouldn't want to impose." And going into his house felt like stepping too far into his life.

He moved under the light. "I'll bet Kate is having the time of her life. If you come back too soon, she'll be disappointed." He gestured. "Come in, please. We can't talk with you hovering on the doorstep."

He was probably right about Kate. She stepped into the tiny hallway, and he closed the door behind her.

''In here.'' He ushered her through an archway on the right. ''Make yourself comfortable. I have coffee brewing.''

Before she could protest, he'd vanished through the door at the back of the hall. She shrugged, turned to the archway, and stopped in surprise. Whatever she'd expected of Mitch's house, it wasn't this.

Pale yellow walls and warm wooden wainscoting set off a living room that might have appeared in a country living magazine. The room was brightened with chintz; braided rugs accented the wide-paneled wooden floors. A fire burned cheerfully in the brick fireplace. It certainly didn't look like any bachelor's apartment she'd ever imagined.

She crossed slowly to the fireplace. It took a moment to realize what was missing. There were no family pictures. Mitch had a family-oriented room without any hint of family. In fact, only one photo graced the mantel. She moved closer, holding out her hands to the blaze, and looked at it.

Mitch, Brett and Alex. She should have expected that. They couldn't have been much more than high school age in the picture, but she recognized each of them at first glance. The photo had been taken outdoors, with the three of them lined up on a log.

''Looking at the three monkeys?'' China mugs rattled on a tray as Mitch came in with the coffee. He put the tray on the coffee table and came to stand next to her.

Too close, that was all she could think. He stood

too close for her peace of mind. He was dressed as casually as she'd ever seen him, in jeans and a cream sweater that made his skin glow. She couldn't breathe without inhaling the faint musky scent of his after-shave lotion.

She forced herself to concentrate on his words. "Why three monkeys? You mean like 'hear no evil'?"

"Something like that. It's what Brett always calls that picture."

Something almost sad touched his eyes as he looked at it, and she found herself wanting to know why. "You were pretty young there, weren't you?"

"Teenagers." He shrugged. "Thought we had the world by the tail, like most kids that age."

He gestured toward the couch, and she sat, then wished she'd taken the chair instead. He left a foot between them when he sat beside her, but it was still too close.

Businesslike, she reminded herself. *You want to get things back on a nice, businesslike basis.*

Then he smiled at her over his coffee mug, and her heart thumped out of rhythm. They were alone together. Maybe she should have brought the baby, as a sort of buffer between her and Mitch.

"I really am sorry." She hurried into speech, because it seemed safer than sitting in silence.

"Forget it."

"Have you?"

"No," he replied.

She met his gaze, startled, and he gave her a rueful smile.

"I decided I'd better not forget it, because I think you're right."

That smile was doing such odd things to her that she wasn't sure she could say anything intelligible. Luckily, he didn't seem to expect anything.

"I've been sitting here going over it. Trying to be angry." He frowned into the flames. "Instead, I kept seeing Davey's face, thinking about his family. Wondering if you're right about me." He shrugged. "It would account for a lot."

"Your family…" She stopped, remembering the unpleasant things Enid had said about his family. About him.

His face seemed to freeze. "I could never count on my family for anything."

"I'm sorry." It seemed to be all she could say.

He reached forward, picking up a poker to shove a log into place. The flames leaped, casting flickering shadows on the strong planes of his face.

"When I look at Davey, I guess I see the kid I was. Running the streets with no one who cared enough to make me behave myself."

Maybe it was safer to keep the focus on Davey, instead of on Mitch. "Does Davey have anyone?" she asked.

"Just his father." His expression eased slightly. He'd probably much rather talk about Davey than himself. He leaned elbows on his knees, letting the poker dangle. "Ed Flagler doesn't mistreat the boy, as far as we can tell. He just doesn't pay attention to him. Davey's headed for trouble if something doesn't change."

Obviously she'd been wrong. He did care what happened to the boy.

"You're planning to talk to the father. Do you think you can get through to him? Make him see the damage he's doing to his son?"

"It's worth a try." His mouth tightened into a grim, painful line. "At least he's still there. That counts for something."

Pain gripped her heart suddenly, but it wasn't for Davey. It was for Mitch. He betrayed so clearly the lonely boy he'd been. Maybe he still hadn't admitted to himself how much his father's leaving had hurt him.

This house—she glanced at the room with new eyes. Mitch hadn't just bought a place because he was tired of renting. He'd created a home here—the home he'd never had before.

She cleared her throat, trying to suppress the tears that choked her. "If talking to the father doesn't do any good, what will you do about Davey?"

"Guess I can't just throw him in a cell." He sent a sideways glance at her. "Some smart lawyer would probably get after me if I did that."

"Probably," she agreed.

"So I'm going to put him to work."

"Work? Isn't he kind of young for that?"

He shrugged. "Never too early to learn the value of work, especially for a kid like Davey. I figure I'll offer to pay him for doing some odd jobs around the station, maybe even around here. That might make him see he doesn't have to steal if he wants something."

He understood the child better than she'd thought. He was going to a lot of trouble for Davey.

"Better watch out. He might start looking up to you."

His mouth quirked. "That'll be the day. Far as he's concerned, I'm the enemy."

"It's pretty obvious the boy needs a role model. Maybe he's found one."

Some emotion she couldn't identify shadowed his eyes. "I'm not setting myself up to be a substitute father. With the example my father set for me, I don't know how."

There wasn't anything she could say to that, was there? But it was pretty clear that her goal of getting things back to a businesslike basis between them was doomed to failure.

The pain in her heart for the lonely boy who lurked inside him told her she'd already started to care too much.

What was the matter with him? He was saying things he'd never said to a living soul. Not even to Alex, though Alex probably guessed most of it. Somehow in a few short days, Anne Morden had managed to touch a part of him he'd closed off a long time ago.

She looked as if she didn't know what to say. *Change the subject,* that was what he had to do. Get off the painful topic that touched too close to his heart.

He nodded toward the mantel photo of himself with Brett and Alex. "That picture was actually taken on the trip I started to tell you about today."

"Trip? Oh, you mean the incident Alex mentioned."

"Our adventure." He felt his voice get lighter as he steered away from the painful subject of fatherhood.

"I'm almost afraid to ask what kind of adventure, especially since Alex seems to think you saved his life."

He shook his head. "Alex exaggerated. If anything, he saved my life. Or maybe we all saved each other's lives."

Anne picked up her coffee mug and leaned back. The plain gold band she wore on her right hand winked in the firelight. "That sounds like a story."

Probably she was as glad as he was to get off painful subjects. "Our senior camping trip. The three of us were assigned to work together. We were orienteering—you know, finding our way in the woods with just a map and a compass."

"I know. Believe it or not, I went to summer

camp once upon a time. I can even build a camp-fire.''

"You get the idea, then. We were supposed to find our way to a meeting point. Trouble was, no-body'd counted on Brett losing the map. Or on a torrential rainstorm. The three of us ended up trapped in a quarry with the water rising.'' Amazing that he could smile about it now. "It was like every bad disaster movie you ever saw.''

"It doesn't sound like much fun to me. How can you joke about it?''

"You know what teenage boys are like. We thought we were indestructible. Right up until the moment we realized we might not get out.''

He'd been making light of it, but all of a sudden the memory got a little too real. He felt the cold rain pelting his face, felt the wind threatening to rip his slicker from his back. Felt his hands slipping from cold wet rock.

"What did you do?''

"First we blamed each other. Then we fought about how we were going to get out.''

"That sounds predictable.''

"That almost got Alex killed.''

In an instant he was back in the quarry, grasping Alex's hand as the water pulled at him. His hand slipping, muscles screaming…

"What happened?''

"Brett and I managed to get him onto a rock.'' They'd huddled, drenched, clinging to each other, sensing death was only a misstep away. "That got us smart in a hurry. We prayed. And we realized working together was the only way we'd ever get out."

He'd never forget the next few hours. They'd struggled up the rock face, helping each other, goading each other on. They'd finally reached the top, exhausted but alive.

"No wonder you've stayed close all this time. It changed your lives."

She was too perceptive. She saw right through him, saw the things he didn't say.

"I guess it did." His voice had gone husky, and he cleared his throat. "Before that, I figured people were right about me, so what was the use of trying? Afterward...well, it seemed that if God bothered to pull me out of that quarry, He expected something from me."

"That's when you went into the military?"

He nodded. "Nobody needed me here." She probably knew he was thinking of his family, disintegrated completely by that time, thanks to his father.

She reached toward him, as if to offer comfort. But when her hand touched his, something far more vivid than comfort flashed between them.

Firelight reflected in the eyes that met his—wide, aware.

He shouldn't. But he couldn't help it. He leaned forward until his lips met hers.

The kiss was tentative at first, and then he felt her breath catch. Her lips softened against his. He drew her closer, inhaling the warm sweet scent of her. He didn't want this to end.

Her hands pushed against his chest, and he released her instantly.

She drew back, cheeks flushing, eyes not quite meeting his. "I think I'd better go." She shot off the couch.

Choking down his disappointment, he nodded.

He could try to pretend it hadn't happened, but that wouldn't work. He'd blown it. This time he'd really blown it. He'd given in to the need to hold her, and now she'd never want him near her again.

Chapter Eight

~❧~

Mitch shoved his desk chair away from the computer hard enough to hit the wall. Why wasn't he finding anything on the elusive Marcy Brown? It was as if the woman had vanished off the face of the earth.

Wanda would probably do this search better than he could, but he wasn't about to involve her in it. No, he'd just have to struggle on and hope he didn't drive himself crazy before he came up with something.

He couldn't kid himself that his current state of frustration had much to do with his lack of success. The problem gnawing his gut and tangling his nerves was a lot more personal than that: Anne, and last night's kiss.

How had he let himself do that? In fact, how had

he let the entire situation happen? He'd told Anne things about himself that he'd never told anyone else, and what he hadn't told her she'd guessed. And then he'd capped his indiscretion by kissing the one woman in the world he should have had sense enough to keep his hands off.

The trouble was, he'd let himself become attracted to Anne. He frowned at the chair where she'd sat that first day, when she'd dropped her bombshell into his life. She'd been an unwelcome intrusion, maybe even a threat. Now…

Now she'd become important to him. But even if it hadn't been for the complication of Emilie's parentage, she was out of his league. And even if none of that existed, there would still be an impenetrable barrier between them. All she wanted was a family, and that was the one thing he'd decided a long time ago that he'd never have.

His fists clenched on the arms of the chair. *The apple doesn't fall far from the tree. Those Donovans are all alike.* You hear that often enough when you are a kid, you get the message. He wouldn't risk being the kind of father his had been.

He reached toward the keyboard. *Find Marcy Brown.* That was the only useful thing he could do.

The telephone rang. He frowned, snatching it up. Hadn't he told Wanda not to disturb him?

''Mitch, Wanda said you were busy, so don't you go blaming her.'' Kate sounded more flustered than usual. "I just had to talk to you, and I've got to leave in a few minutes."

"Leave? Where are you going?" Kate never left the bed-and-breakfast when she had a guest. It was unheard of.

"My sister's had a bad fall, maybe broken her hip." Kate's voice trembled on the verge of tears. "I just don't know, at her age, what we'll do if it's broken." She took an audible breath. "I've got to go, right now."

"Of course you do," he soothed. "I'm sure Anne won't mind moving to another bed-and-breakfast, under the circumstances."

"Well, we've got that taken care of. Anne says she'd rather stay here, since she's got the baby settled and all. There's plenty of food in the kitchen, and she says they'll be just fine."

"Then you don't have to worry, do you? You just get on to your sister's and call if there's anything you need."

"That's just it. I need your help."

"You've got it." Kate surely knew by now that she could count on him.

"I want you to look in on Anne and the baby. Promise me, now."

"I'm sure Anne..."

Doesn't want me looking in on her. That's what he wanted to say, but he couldn't.

"Please." Worry laced Kate's voice. "Anne

didn't feel well when she came in last night, I could tell. I want you to check on them."

If Anne hadn't felt well, it was probably because of what had happened between them, but he could hardly say that to Kate.

"All right. I promise I'll look in on Anne and the baby."

And somehow or other I'll keep my hands off her and my feelings in check.

"Are you sure you're going to be all right?" Kate hovered at the door, car keys in hand, a worried expression on her face.

"We'll be fine," Anne said for what seemed the tenth time. Kate's worries about her sister were undoubtedly spilling over onto everyone else. She balanced Emilie on one hip and gave Kate a reassuring smile. "We're used to being by ourselves, don't forget."

"You've been looking a little pale since last night." Kate frowned. "Are you sure…"

"I'm fine." *Except for a monster of a headache and the feeling I've made a complete fool of myself.* "You go on. And if there's anything else you want me to do here, just call and let me know."

Kate nodded, finally edging her way out the door. "Mitch will be by to see if you need anything. He promised."

She felt the smile stiffen on her face. "He doesn't have to do that."

"I'll feel better if he does." Kate turned, waved bye-bye to Emilie, and started down the steps. Apparently the thought that Mitch was in charge gave her enough confidence to leave.

Anne closed the door and leaned against it. The last thing she needed or wanted was to have Mitch checking up on her. After last night's fiasco, she didn't know how she'd manage to look him in the eye.

What had gotten into her? She'd practically invited him to kiss her. And when he had, she'd bolted like a scared rabbit.

She hadn't been prepared for the devastating effect of his lips on hers—that was the truth of the matter. She'd been involved in the closeness of the moment, responding to his openness with her. She'd told herself they were becoming friends. The next moment they'd touched, and she'd known this was something much more powerful than simple friendship.

She rubbed her temples wearily. Maybe if she could get rid of this headache, she could think about the whole subject rationally. Her cheeks felt hot, and her ability to reason seemed to have vanished. Emilie's teething had given her a restless night and too much wakeful time remembering that moment in Mitch's arms.

"How about a nap?" She stroked the baby's cheek. "Okay? Emilie will take a nap and Mommy will, too. Then we'll both feel better."

And then maybe she could get her composure back in place before she saw Mitch again.

It was nearly suppertime, and none of those things had happened. Emilie fussed, chewing restlessly on a teething biscuit, then throwing it on the floor. The fourth time Anne picked it up, she decided her head would probably explode if she bent over one more time.

You couldn't get sick if you were a single parent. She'd come to that realization at some point in the last few months. You just couldn't, not unless you had a reliable baby-sitter on tap. At home in Philadelphia there were a half-a-dozen people she could call.

But she wasn't at home, and the only person she knew well enough to call in Bedford Creek was the one person she definitely would not call.

She bounced the wailing baby on her hip and started down the stairs. She'd better get the teething ring she'd put in the refrigerator to chill. Maybe that would soothe Emilie.

A wave of dizziness hit her halfway down. She sat abruptly, clutching Emilie, and leaned her head against the rail.

"It's all right." She patted Emilie, wishing someone would say that to her. "It's going to be all right. We're fine."

The knock on the door sounded far away, too far

away for her to do anything about it. Maybe whoever it was would just go away.

Thirty seconds later the door clicked open. Mitch appeared in the hallway. "Anne?" He looked, then took the steps two at a time and knelt beside her. "What is it? What's wrong?"

"Nothing." She made a valiant effort to straighten up. "I'm fine."

"Funny, you don't look fine. Your cheeks are beet red, and your eyes are glazed."

"Thanks," she muttered. She should have been offended, but it took too much effort.

He put his hand on her forehead. His palm felt so cool. She just wanted him to leave it there until the throbbing in her temples went away.

"You're running a fever." He touched Emilie's cheek. "What about the baby? Is she sick, too?"

She struggled to concentrate. Okay, she was sick. No wonder she felt so bad. "Just teething, I think."

"Come here, little girl." He lifted Emilie from her arms. "Are you feeling cranky? Let's give Mommy a rest."

To her astonishment, Emilie's wails ceased. The silence was welcoming.

"Thank you." She forced herself to focus. "If you could just bring me her teething ring and a bottle, maybe I can get her settled."

"Settled? You don't look capable of picking up a marshmallow, let alone a baby." His arm went around her. "Come on. I'll help you to bed."

She couldn't resist leaning against that strong arm, even though she knew she shouldn't. "I'm fine, really I am."

"I know." He sounded amused. "You can do it yourself. But this time you can't, literally."

He stood, taking her with him, apparently not having a problem carrying the baby and lugging her, too. She forced herself to put one foot in front of the other, aware Mitch was almost carrying her.

When they reached the suite, he plopped Emilie in her playpen, to which she immediately objected. Anne winced at her cries and reached for her.

"No, you don't." Mitch steered her toward the bedroom. "The last thing that baby needs is to get whatever bug you have. Do you want me to call a doctor for you?"

She shook her head, the movement making her wince again. "It's probably just the twenty-four-hour virus Kate says has been going around. I'll be fine, honestly."

"After you get some rest." He half carried her to the bed and sat her down. "Don't worry. I'll take care of Emilie."

She wanted to object, but the bed felt so good after a mostly sleepless night. She slid down bonelessly, her head coming to rest on the cool, smooth pillow.

"Just a little nap," she murmured. "Then I'll be fine."

"I'll bring you some water." Mitch pulled up the

quilt and tucked it around her gently. Her eyes closed. She thought she felt his fingers touch her cheek, and then she heard him move away.

Just a short nap, that was all she needed. She slid rapidly toward sleep. Just a short nap.

The baby was still crying. Well, one thing at a time. Mitch crossed to the playpen and picked up Emilie. This time no magic happened—she continued to wail, although the volume decreased.

"Okay, little girl, it's okay." He bounced her on his hip the way he'd seen Anne do when she fussed.

"Everything's going to be all right. Mitch will take care of you."

Yeah, right. It was one thing to give a baby a bottle and then hand it back when it cried. Taking complete care of one was something else entirely.

Emilie seemed a little calmer when he talked, so he did his thinking out loud. "I guess I could call somebody else to help. Wanda, maybe."

It seemed to be working. The baby's sobs quieted to whimpers, and she looked up into his face.

"But do I really want to do that? Open us up to her curiosity? No, I don't think so."

Besides, he'd told Anne he'd take care of them.

"So I guess you're stuck with me." He smiled at Emilie. She smiled back, and he felt as if he'd struck gold. "Let's get some water for your mommy, and we'll look for that teething ring she mentioned."

He tickled Emilie, getting a belly laugh that startled and amused him, then headed for the kitchen.

It was harder than it looked to manipulate a glass of ice water, a bottle of aspirin and a baby. He didn't want to put her down, because she might start crying again. He had an uneasy suspicion that if she did, he wouldn't find it so easy to stop her.

"Okay." He stuffed the aspirin bottle in his back pocket and set the water pitcher back in the refrigerator with his free hand. "Let's get this up to Mommy. Maybe I'll have to ask her where the teething thing is."

He started to close the door, then realized that pink, gel-filled donut looked out of place in Kate's refrigerator. "Hey, is this yours?" He held it out to Emilie, who grabbed it and stuffed it in her mouth. "I guess so."

He picked up the glass. "One more time up the stairs, okay?"

Emilie seemed content to be put in her playpen now that she had the teething ring to chew on, so he deposited her and tiptoed into the bedroom.

Anne lay on her side, one hand under the pillow. Her black hair tumbled about her face, curling damply on her neck. He brushed it back, resisting the urge to let his fingers linger against her soft cheek.

"Anne." He hated to disturb her, but she probably should take something for the fever.

She stirred, and her eyes opened, focusing on him.

"I brought you some aspirin and a glass of water."

She nodded, propping herself on one elbow long enough to down the tablets with a thirsty gulp of water. "Emilie…"

"Emilie's fine. I found the teething ring, but you'd better tell me what to feed her and when."

"I'll get up." She started to push the quilt aside, and he tucked it back over her firmly.

"No, you're not getting up. I can feed Emilie. Just tell me what I need to know."

She sank back on the pillow, apparently realizing she wasn't going anywhere very soon. "The baby food's down on the kitchen counter. Give her—" she frowned, as if trying to concentrate "—give her something with meat and a fruit. That'll be fine for now."

Her eyes drifted closed.

Which fruit? he wanted to ask. *What about a bottle?*

But already she'd slid into sleep, her breath soft and even, her lashes dark against pale skin. She looked vulnerable, and he had a ridiculous urge to protect her. He shook his head. In such a short time she'd touched some tender place in his soul, and he wasn't sure how he was going to get her back out again.

Mitch went quietly back out to the living room of the suite and looked down at Emilie, who was gnawing on the teething ring. "Well, I guess it's just you and me, kid. Tell you what, you cooperate, and we'll get along just fine.''

Supper, he decided. Feed her, and then she'd go to sleep, right? He carried her down to the kitchen.

Luckily, Kate had already set up a high chair. Unluckily, Emilie didn't seem to want to go into it. She stiffened her legs, lunging backward in his arms.

"Come on, sweetheart. A little cooperation here.''

Emilie didn't agree. Trying to put her in the high chair was like trying to fold an iron bar.

He'd seen Anne put some small crackers on the tray when they'd been in the café. Maybe that would work. He gazed around the kitchen, looking for inspiration. He found a small box of crackers stacked with the jars of baby food. Quickly he shook a few onto the tray.

"Look, Emilie. You like these.''

She stopped in mid-cry at the sight.

Holding his breath, he slid her into the high chair. She snatched one of the crackers and stuffed it in her mouth.

"Okay, one problem solved.'' He fastened the strap around her waist, then turned to the array of baby food on the counter. "Let's see what looks good.''

Actually, as far as he was concerned, none of it looked good. He reminded himself that he wasn't eight months old. Maybe to Emilie this stuff looked like filet mignon.

He heated up the chicken-and-rice mixture.

"Here we go, Emilie." He shoveled a spoonful of chicken into her mouth.

She smiled, and most of the chicken spilled right back out of her mouth, landing down the front of her ruffled pink outfit.

Half an hour later Emilie was liberally sprinkled with chicken, rice and pears, to say nothing of the cracker crumbs. Also well adorned were Mitch's shirt, the high chair and the floor. The way things had gone, it wouldn't surprise him if some of the chicken had found its way into the house next door.

"Maybe we're done." He lifted her cautiously from the chair, holding her at arm's length, a new admiration for Anne filling him. She did this every day, and she didn't have anyone to spell her.

"Okay, let's get you cleaned up." He glanced at his shirt. "Me, too."

He carried her upstairs and eased open the door to the bedroom. Anne slept, still curled on her side. He tiptoed to the bed and touched her forehead. Her skin seemed a little cooler than it had earlier, unless he was imagining things.

Okay, he could do this. He carried Emilie into the bathroom. He looked at the tub, then shook his head. No way. Emilie would do with a sponge bath tonight.

By the time they were finished, Emilie was clean and he was wet. He bundled her into a sleeper and carried her out to the playpen. She settled without a murmur.

He stretched out on the couch, wedging one of the small pillows under his head. He closed his eyes. Peace, heavenly peace…

Sometime later a piercing wail split the air. He catapulted off the couch, heart pounding. Emilie. He reached her in a second, bent to scoop her up.

"Hey, it's okay. Don't cry."

The wail went up in volume and in pitch. Anne would never be able to sleep through this, would she?

But apparently she could.

"Shh, Emilie, it's all right. Don't cry, okay?" He felt like crying himself. If there was a more helpless sensation in the world than this, he didn't know what it was.

"It's all right. Honest." He bounced her, walking across to the windows, then back.

Strangely enough, that seemed to soothe her. The wails decreased. He settled her against his chest and turned to walk the length of the room again. Maybe he could walk her back to sleep, then get some rest himself.

That was only half right. Emilie dozed against his chest, her head nestled into the curve of his neck. But the instant he tried to put her down, her eyes popped open and the wail started again.

Okay, that wouldn't work. Looked like he'd have to keep walking.

This wasn't so bad, was it? He circled the room for the twentieth time or so. He'd walked guard duty longer than this and been more tired. He could do it. It might not be the way he'd pick to spend this evening, but he could do it.

His father's face flickered briefly in his mind, and he banished it instantly. He didn't think about Ken Donovan, not anymore.

But his father wouldn't have put in a night like this—not in a million years.

Chapter Nine

Anne came awake slowly, pushing herself upward from fathoms-deep sleep. Something was wrong, and for a moment she couldn't think what it was. Then she realized it was the first morning in months Emilie hadn't wakened her.

She shot upright in the bed, then grabbed her head. The headache had disappeared, replaced by the sensation that her head was about to drift off into space. Slowly, cautiously, she swung her feet over the side of the bed.

Mitch had been here, hadn't he? Or had she dreamed it? No, of course she hadn't. Mitch hurrying in the door, helping her up to bed, saying he'd take care of Emilie.

The crib was empty. Where was Emilie?

She forced herself to her feet and stumbled to the door, yanked it open. Emilie—

Mitch lay on the floor, sleeping. He cradled Emilie between his arms. She slept, too, her head pillowed on Mitch's chest. His strong hands held her firmly even in sleep.

She could fall in love with this man.

The realization hit her like a kick to the heart, followed immediately by a wave of panic. What was she thinking? She didn't intend to fall in love with anyone, certainly not with Mitch.

She tiptoed across the rug and reached for Emilie. Her touch was so gentle that the baby didn't wake, but Mitch's arms tightened instantly. His eyes flickered open, warming when he saw her. He smiled.

Her breath seemed to stop. She wanted to reach out to him, to touch the firm lines of his face, to wipe away all the reserve that hid his feelings. She wanted...

She took a step back. This was dangerous. She couldn't let herself feel this way.

"Good morning. Feeling better?" Mitch shifted position, and Emilie woke. She cooed, patting Mitch with both small hands.

"I'm fine. Really." Anne reached for the baby. "Let me take her. Goodness, I never expected you to stay all night. You should have wakened me."

He grinned. "That would have taken an earthquake. Besides, we got along fine." He stood, still holding the baby. "I'm not sure you should be up yet. You look a little dizzy."

"I just need a shower to clear my head. Then I'll

be okay. Really, you don't have to do anything else. I'm sure it's time for you to get ready for work.'' And the sooner he was out of here, the sooner her breathing would return to normal.

He glanced at his watch. ''It's early yet. Suppose I take Emilie downstairs and start some breakfast while you get that shower. Then we'll see how you feel.''

Anne would have argued, but he was already out the door with Emilie. Short of chasing him down the stairs, there wasn't much she could do. And a shower might clear her head and help her get rid of thoughts about Mitch that didn't go anywhere.

Standing under the hot spray helped her body, but it didn't seem to be doing much for the rest of her. Her heart and mind still felt jumbled with confused feelings. She couldn't—shouldn't—feel anything for Mitch under these difficult circumstances.

She tilted her head back, letting the water run down her face. After Terry's death, she'd made a deliberate decision that she'd never marry again. Maybe she wasn't cut out for marriage; maybe she just didn't have the capacity for closeness that it required.

It might be different with someone like Mitch. The thought slipped into her mind and refused to be dislodged.

By the time she dried her hair and pulled on a sweater and slacks the light-headedness had eased. She certainly wouldn't be running any marathons today, but she could take care of Emilie. Mitch was probably itching to get out of here.

The picture that met her eyes when she entered the kitchen didn't suggest any desire on Mitch's part to run out the door. He was spooning cereal into Emilie's mouth, sipping at a mug of coffee between bites. Both of them seemed perfectly content. Mitch looked too casually attractive with a slight stubble of beard darkening his face.

"You didn't need to do that. I can feed her."

"Hey, I'm just getting good at this." He caught a bubble of cereal that spilled out of Emilie's mouth when she smiled. "And this time I remembered the bib."

The coffee's aroma lured her to the counter, where she poured a steaming mug. "You tried to feed her without a bib? That must have been messy." She should have told him that when she'd explained about the food, but her mind had been so foggy, it was a wonder she'd said anything coherent at all.

"Messy isn't the word for it. We both needed a complete washup afterward, to say nothing of the kitchen."

Guilt flooded her. Emilie was her responsibility, not his. "You should have wakened me."

"Really?" He lifted an eyebrow, and amusement flickered in those chocolate-brown eyes. "If Emilie's screaming didn't wake you up, I don't think I could have."

"I'm so sorry." Embarrassment heated her cheeks. "I never should have…"

"What? Gotten sick? Give yourself a break, Anne. You're not some kind of superwoman."

"I know, but I still feel guilty leaving Emilie to you when she's teething and miserable."

He paused, spoon half in Emilie's mouth, looking at the baby intently. "If that clink I just heard means anything, the teething problem might be solved for the moment."

"Really?" She hurried around the table and bent over Emilie. "Let Mommy see, sweetheart." She rubbed Emilie's gum, feeling the sharp edge of a tooth. "Look at that! Emilie got a new tooth."

Mitch's smile took in both of them. "Good going, Emilie."

The baby cooed. The image of the three of them, smiling at each other, seemed to solidify in Anne's mind. It might almost be the picture of…a family.

She blinked rapidly. She shouldn't think things like that. "I can finish feeding her."

"No, you can sit down and eat something, so you won't almost pass out on me again. How about some cereal? An egg?"

Actually, she did feel a bit hollow inside. "Maybe a piece of toast."

Mitch reached out to put two slices of bread in the toaster. "Will you please sit down? You're making me nervous."

"I didn't really pass out." Her memory of those

moments on the stairs was a little fuzzy, but she was sure of that. She sank into the chair he pushed out for her. "I'm grateful you came in just then. I'm not sure what we'd have done without your help."

"Kate made me promise to check on you two. I guess she knew what she was doing." He scooped the last spoonful of cereal from the bowl and offered it to Emilie, but she turned her head away.

"Better stop there," Anne advised, grinning. "Her next move will be to swat the spoon, and you'll be coping with flying cereal."

"You're the mommy. I guess you know best." He set the bowl on the table. "Anything else I should give her?"

"Let her work on that bottle of juice." He'd turned her thanks away so easily that she felt compelled to say something more. "I want you to know how much I appreciate your help. Getting sick is a big problem when you're a single parent. You don't have anyone to spell you."

He nodded. "Believe me, sometime in the wee hours I got the picture. Parents should come in sets, if possible." His smile turned into a searching look. "I guess you and your husband must really have wanted a family."

It was a natural assumption. She was tempted to let it stand, but that seemed wrong.

"I don't think having a family was ever part of Terry's idea of marriage. He saw us as the classic yuppie couple—two jobs, no kids." Her mouth twisted a little. "He never seemed to want more than that. Two busy professionals with no time for kids and not much time for each other."

She hadn't intended to say that much, and surprise at her candor mingled with embarrassment.

His hand covered hers for a brief moment, sending a flood of warmth along her skin. "I guess that's why you feel the way you do about Emilie."

"She means everything to me." She blinked back the tears that suddenly filled her eyes.

Emilie, apparently feeling she'd been out of the conversation long enough, pounded her bottle on the tray. "Ma, ma, ma, ma, ma!"

"The experts say that's babbling, but I think it's 'Mama.'" Anne covered her ears in mock dismay at the onslaught of noise. "Oh, Emilie, stop."

Mitch caught the flailing bottle, closing his large hand around Emilie's small one. "Hey, little one, enough."

Emilie fastened her wide blue gaze on him. "Da, da, da, da, da!" she shouted.

Anne didn't know which of them was the more embarrassed. Mitch's cheeks reddened beneath his tanned skin and hers felt as if they were on fire.

"It's just nonsense syllables," she said quickly. "She doesn't know what they mean." Embarrassment made her rush to fill the silence with words. "Not that you wouldn't—I mean, I'm sure you'd make a great father." The words slipped out before she had time to think that they might not be wise.

His face tightened until it resembled the mask he'd put on against her that first afternoon in his office.

"I guess that's something I'll never know. I decided a long time ago I wasn't cut out for fatherhood."

She must have murmured something, but she wasn't sure what. She was glad she hadn't believed in that image she'd had of the three of them as a family. For a lot of reasons, it was clearly impossible.

Mitch's office was his refuge. Trouble was, it didn't seem to keep out thoughts of Anne.

Her vulnerability. Her strength. Her determination to take care of the child she saw as hers.

He'd tried to tell himself that last night was nothing—or at least, the sort of thing he'd do for anyone. But he couldn't. It was just too tempting. He'd been part of their lives last night, hers and Emilie's. He'd been important to them in a personal way—not as a cop, but as a husband, a father, would be.

One night. He shoved his chair away from the desk. It had only been a few short hours. Maybe he'd held up to that, but in the long run, there were no guarantees he wouldn't turn out to be just like his father. He wouldn't wish that on any kid.

The sound of raised voices in the outer office interrupted the uncomfortable thoughts. He opened the door to find Wanda and Davey glaring at each other, toe to toe.

Wanda turned the glare on Mitch. "You were the one who hired this twerp. Are you going to let him get away with this?"

He suppressed a sigh. "Maybe I could tell you, if I knew what he'd done."

Wanda flung out her hand toward the big front window. "I told him to wash the window. Did he do it? No! He messed around and let the cleaner dry on the window, and now it looks worse than it did before. He ought to be paying me if I have to clean up after him."

"You're not going to clean up after him."

"Go ahead, take her side. I figured you would." Davey threw down the roll of paper towels. "I'm getting out of here."

Mitch grabbed the kid. The look in the boy's eyes was familiar. He knew what that feeling was, because he'd been there himself. It was wanting someone to care whether he'd done something right or not, and being afraid of that wanting.

"Davey's going to do it again, and this time he'll get it right. That's what I'm paying him for."

"What if I don't want your stupid old job?"

This was familiar, too. He knew what it was like to want to bite someone for taking an interest.

"You don't have a choice, remember? Your father and I agreed you'd work for me, and I'd forget the little incident with the package." Anne would probably call it blackmail, but if it worked, it was worth it.

"All right, all right!" Davey snatched up the roll of towels. "I'll do your stupid windows, but then I gotta get home for supper."

"If he's going to do that window, you can stay right here and watch him." Wanda planted her hands on her hips. "Baby-sitting isn't in my job description."

"Baby-sitting! Who you calling a baby?"

Mitch gestured Wanda toward her desk and turned Davey to the window. He wasn't going to give up on the kid, not this easily.

But what had happened to the quiet life he'd had before Anne walked into it?

The late afternoon sun warmed the air enough to flirt with spring as Anne pushed the stroller up Main Street. Getting out for a while was a good idea. She'd hung around the house until she'd begun to drive herself crazy.

Thinking about Mitch too much, remembering those moments in the kitchen this morning—she couldn't dwell on it. There wasn't anything between them and there never would be, because he was determined to avoid the very thing that had become the most important in the world to her.

So she wasn't going to think about it anymore. She and Emilie would enjoy the sunshine, she'd pick up a few things at the grocery store, and they'd have a cozy supper, just the two of them. They didn't need anyone else.

"Ms. Morden! How nice to see you out and about. I heard you were sick."

Pastor Richie hurried down the sidewalk, beaming at her.

"I'm fine now, thank you." And how on earth had he heard about it so quickly? "Just one of those twenty-four-hour viruses, I guess."

He shook his head. "Nasty things going around." He bent to pat Emilie's cheek. "This beautiful little one didn't get anything, I hope."

"Nothing but a brand-new tooth." She couldn't help sounding like a proud mama some of the time.

"Well, isn't that nice." His round, cherubic face grew a bit serious. "Have you had any luck with your efforts to find that young lady you were looking for?"

"No, not yet. Mitch is checking out some leads."

"I looked back over the roster of the singles group for that time, and it jogged my memory. Ellie Wayne was a member then, and I believe those girls hit it off. She might have stayed in touch."

Anne's pulse jumped a notch at the possibility. "Is this Ellie Wayne still in town?"

"Goodness, yes. She runs the gift shop just the other side of the police station. Would you like me to ask her about the girl?"

"Thanks, but I'll do it." She couldn't help the size of her smile, which probably betrayed the fact that her interest was far from casual. "That's so nice of you. Thank you."

"My pleasure." He beamed at them both impartially. "Will I see you in church this Sunday?"

"Yes, of course. We're looking forward to worshiping with you. I hope the baby's not a problem."

He patted Emilie's cheek again. "How could she possibly be a problem? We have a nursery, but if you feel more comfortable keeping her with you, that's fine."

How much was she giving away to his wise eyes? He seemed to guess or to know more than she'd said.

"Thank you. We'll see you Sunday, then."

A lead, at last, she thought, pushing the stroller forward with renewed energy. And it was one she could follow up herself. She didn't need to involve Mitch at all, which was probably for the best.

She walked on down the street. Many of the shops were closed, probably until spring. She looked up at the mountain ridge. The faintest greenish haze seemed to cover it—not spring, but maybe a hint of it.

The bell over the gift shop door tinkled as she lifted the stroller up the step from the street. The mingled aroma of herbs, dried flowers and candles swept over her.

"Help you?" The woman behind the counter wore her thick dark hair in twin braids that swung almost to her waist. She had a strong, intelligent face, innocent of makeup, and a welcoming smile.

"Just looking."

Anne lifted the baby into her arms. Trying to push the stroller along the narrow, crowded aisles would be a recipe for disaster.

"Are you interested in something special?"

She glanced around. It would probably be diplomatic to buy something. "I'd like a dried-flower arrangement. Something with mauve and blue in it."

"This way." The woman came out from behind the counter. "You're Chief Donovan's friend, aren't you? Staying at The Willows?"

She couldn't get away from the mention of him, not in this town. She nodded. "Anne Morden."

"Ellie Wayne." She touched Emilie's hand. "What a beautiful baby."

"I think Pastor Richie mentioned your name to me. We were talking about a...well, a friend of a friend who used to be in the singles group with you. Marcy Brown. Do you remember her?"

Ellie nodded, her eyes assessing Anne.

"I just wondered if you happened to have her current address."

"Why do you want it?" Ellie's question was blunt.

"We had a mutual friend who passed away a few months ago. I wanted to let her know." And ask her some questions, too.

"I'm sorry." Ellie's eyes darkened with sympathy. "I have an address from a Christmas card, if that'll do you any good. I think she was moving, but her mail might still be forwarded. So I guess a letter could reach her."

"I'd really appreciate it." A few-months'-old address was better than nothing.

"I'll get it for you."

As the woman moved away, the bell on the door jingled.

Anne turned. Mitch stood in the doorway, and her heart was suddenly thumping loud enough for her to hear.

Chapter Ten

*W*hat exactly is Anne up to now? Mitch had glimpsed her from the window where he was supervising Davey's reluctant cleaning. He'd expected her to turn into the station and had been ridiculously disappointed when she'd gone past. And somewhat surprised when she'd walked into the gift shop.

Her slightly guilty expression told him she was doing something she thought he'd disapprove of—some sleuthing, in other words. If she had some reason to believe Ellie knew something, he wanted in on it.

"I'm helping a customer. I'll be with you in a moment." Ellie gave him a wary look. He didn't think she disliked him; the uniform raised that response in people sometimes. Ellie was generous with others, cautious with him.

"I know." He responded with a bland smile. He turned to Anne. "I'm surprised to see you out already. You must be feeling better."

"Yes, I'm fine." That faint flush in her cheeks probably wasn't from the fever. She was embarrassed at being caught.

"Excuse me, Chief." Ellie brushed past him to lift down a dried-flower wreath, which she held out to Anne. "What about this one?"

Anne touched it gently. "It's beautiful. Did you make all these yourself?"

Ellie smiled at the praise. "And the baskets. Some of the pieces are on consignment from local artists."

Anne had managed to get more out of Ellie in two minutes than Mitch had in two years, he thought. But he didn't think she had come in here just because she liked Ellie's crafts.

"I'll take this one. And I'd love to have that address, if you don't mind writing it down for me."

Ellie glanced from her to Mitch, then nodded. "It'll be in my files in the office. I'll get it."

When she'd disappeared, he lifted an eyebrow at Anne. "Address?"

"It seems she received a Christmas card from Marcy Brown."

"She just happened to volunteer that information?"

"No, of course not. I asked her."

He suppressed a flicker of irritation. "I thought

we agreed you wouldn't go around town asking questions of everyone you meet.''

"I didn't do any such thing." Her eyes snapped. "I happened to run into Pastor Richie, and he suggested I talk with Ellie. Apparently she and Marcy struck up a friendship in the singles group, and he thought they might have been in touch.''

Mitch winced. Looked as if he owed her an apology. Again. "Guess I shouldn't have jumped to conclusions.''

"No, you shouldn't have." She sounded as if she wanted to hold on to her annoyance a bit longer. "And how did you know I was here?''

He gestured toward the station next door. "I was standing at the window, supervising.''

"Supervising what?''

"Davey's window washing.''

He liked the way her face softened at the boy's name. It would be nice to imagine that it did so at the mention of his name, but he doubted it.

"He's been testing the limits to our arrangement, and Wanda refuses to have anything to do with this project.''

She actually smiled. Apparently he was forgiven. "You'll do a better job of it, anyway.''

"I doubt it, but it's nice of you to say so.''

They were standing close together, so close that he could smell the faint, flowery scent she wore. He had to fight the urge to step even closer.

She looked up at him, and her blue eyes seemed to darken. "I'm sure—"

Ellie bustled in from the storeroom or wherever she'd been, her gaze darting from one to the other of them. "Found it." She waved a slip of paper at Anne.

Anne turned to her with what Mitch suspected was relief. "Thank you. I really appreciate this."

The woman shrugged. "No problem. I'll box up the wreath for you."

Ellie busied herself at the far end of the counter, and an uneasy silence grew between him and Anne. What was she thinking? Was she remembering the moment when they'd kissed? Or was she wishing he'd leave her alone?

Anne glanced up at him. "I wouldn't want to keep you from your work."

That seemed to answer the question. He shrugged. "Yeah, I'd better get back to the station. I'll see you tomorrow."

"You will?" She looked startled and not entirely pleased at the thought.

Well, she'd just have to lump it. "I promised Kate a while ago I'd paint the sunroom for her. Davey and I are going to work on it tomorrow, since it's Saturday."

"I see." She managed a smile, but it didn't look particularly genuine. "I'll see you tomorrow, then."

"One more bite, sweetie." Anne spooned cereal into Emilie's mouth as morning sunlight streamed through the kitchen windows. "We need to get you dressed, because Mitch is coming."

Emilie smiled, cereal dribbling onto her chin, just as if she remembered who Mitch was and looked forward to seeing him.

"There. All done." She wiped away the cereal and put the bowl in the sink. Whether or not either of them wanted to see Mitch was beside the point, anyway. He was coming, and she couldn't do anything about it but try and handle his presence better than she had the day before.

That encounter in Ellie's store had been a miserable display. She'd let her confused feelings for Mitch make her uncomfortable and awkward in his presence.

She had to cope with the attraction she felt for him, and she had to do it now. She couldn't go on this way.

Emilie banged on the high chair tray with both fists, as if in emphasis, and Anne lifted her out. She smoothed the fine, silky hair off the baby's forehead.

Maybe the most important question to ask was whether she still believed him to be Emilie's father. She tried to look at it as an attorney, instead of seeing it personally, but she couldn't separate the two.

Anne had grown to know him too well during her time in Bedford Creek. She'd seen the man behind the uniform and the shield, and she liked what she saw.

Integrity. That was the word for it. Every moment she spent with him made her more convinced he was a man of integrity. Every moment lessened her conviction that he was Emilie's father.

She put her cheek against Emilie's soft one. If her father wasn't Mitch, who was it? Time was ticking away, and she didn't seem to be getting anywhere. Was she letting her tangled feelings for Mitch distract her from what was really important here?

Well, if so, that was coming to an end. Regardless of what she might feel for him, the truth was that there would never be anything between them. Everything else aside, Mitch's attitude toward having children made it impossible.

Being Emilie's mother was a full-time job, and giving Emilie the warm, close family relationship Anne had never had herself would fill the empty spaces in her heart. She didn't need or want anything more.

A clatter on the front porch told her the workmen had arrived. Ignoring the way her heart lurched, she went to open the door with Emilie in her arms.

"Good morning." She caught Emilie as the baby made a lunge for Mitch. "I see you're ready to work." She was going to be pleasant, she told herself. She would act as if none of the events of the last few days had happened.

Mitch had a stepladder balanced on one broad shoulder, and he carried two cans of paint in the other hand. His faded jeans had definitely seen better days, as had the T-shirt that stretched across his chest, showing every muscle.

"We'll have the sunroom looking brand-new before you know it." A smile warmed his face, erasing the remnant of annoyance over their last meeting.

A tingle ran along her nerve endings. Her heart didn't seem to have listened to the lecture she'd just given.

She focused on Davey with a welcoming smile. The boy carried a bucket filled with painting gear and wore a disgusted expression. Obviously, this wasn't his idea of the way to spend a Saturday.

She waved toward the sunroom that adjoined Kate's kitchen. "I'll leave you to it. I'll be upstairs getting Emilie dressed if you need anything."

He nodded. "Come on, Davey. This way."

The boy trudged after him down the hall as if headed to his own execution. Suppressing a smile, Anne started up the stairs. Mitch had his work cut out for him in more than painting.

Half an hour later, Anne admitted the truth. She was delaying returning downstairs, delaying seeing Mitch again; she didn't want to put her resolution to the test. But it was time for that to stop. She picked up Emilie and headed downstairs.

"Goodness, you two are fast." They'd already stacked the furniture in the middle of the room and covered it with a drop cloth.

Mitch looked up from opening a can of paint.

"I'm paying this guy by the hour, so I've got to get my money's worth."

"Looks as if you're doing that."

Anne realized Davey's gaze was directed at the baby with a mix of curiosity and trepidation. She smiled at him. "This is Emilie."

He jerked a nod in response, then came closer. "She's pretty little, isn't she?"

"She's almost nine months old." She bounced the baby. "This is Davey, sweetheart."

He took another step closer. "Can she say my name?"

"Probably not. She doesn't say much yet." She tried not to think about the moment when Emilie had looked at Mitch and said "Da-da."

"I never been this close to a baby before." Tentatively, Davey held out one rather dirty hand toward Emilie.

With a happy gurgle, Emilie lunged forward and latched her fist around his finger, smiling.

"Looks as if she likes you," Anne said.

Davey looked at the tiny hand, then up at Anne. "She does, doesn't she?"

A smile spread across his face, changing him from the sullen, angry delinquent into a little boy who liked being liked.

That smile... Her heart warmed at the sight. Somehow seeing a smile like that from the boy made Mitch's efforts seem worthwhile.

"I'm sure she does." She glanced at Mitch. Had he seen what she had?

His gaze met hers and he nodded slightly, as if they shared a secret. The intimacy of his look closed around her heart.

She cleared her throat. "I'll put Emilie in the playpen here in the kitchen. That way she can watch you paint without smelling the fumes. They wouldn't be good for her."

Davey nodded gravely, as if storing that information for possible future use. He detached his finger carefully.

"You watch," he said. "You're going to see some good painting."

He returned to the sunroom with determination. Whether it would last or not she couldn't guess, but it was nice to see.

She plopped Emilie into the playpen, sliding it over so the baby had a view of the sunroom. Emilie seemed to enjoy the unusual activity. She clutched the playpen's mesh and watched every movement with wide blue eyes.

Mitch paused, roller in hand. "Have you heard anything from Kate yet?"

She'd nearly forgotten. "She called last night. It looks as if her sister didn't break her hip, after all. She's badly bruised, so Kate plans to stay and take care of her a bit longer, but she sounded very relieved."

"I'll bet. Kate loves her independence, and I

gather the sister can be pretty bossy at times. Kate will be glad when she can get home again.''

"She asked about you." Actually, Kate had asked if Mitch was taking good care of her. "I told her you'd be coming to paint today. She kept saying you didn't need to do it and she could manage herself."

He grinned. "That's Kate. She's always doing kind things for other people, then is surprised when they want to do something for her."

Was that behind Mitch's friendship with his elderly neighbor? Maybe Kate had been kind to him at a time when he needed kindness.

"She's a good friend," Anne said.

He nodded, smoothing the roller along the wall in a swath of pale yellow. "The first year I came back, she invited me to spend Christmas with her. Alex and his son had gone away, and I didn't have anyone else. She made it sound as if I did her the favor."

Anne leaned against the door frame. "I'm sure she enjoyed it as much as you did."

"She didn't eat as much." He paused, a reminiscent look in his eyes. "She kept saying she loved to see people eat what she'd prepared, so I made her happy."

"Turkey and all the trimmings?"

"What else would you have for Christmas?"

"Hamburger and fries." The words were out before she knew it.

Mitch stared. "Why on earth would your folks serve that?"

It was clearly not the mental image he had of her family life. She shrugged. "They didn't. They'd gone away for the holidays…Gstaad for skiing, I think. The housekeeper didn't want to fix a big dinner just for the two of us, so we hit the burger hut instead."

"Sounds like some of the Christmases I remember as a kid. I always figured other people got the magazine-picture type of Christmas dinner, with the whole family around the table and the father carving a turkey." His voice betrayed the longing he'd probably felt as a child for that kind of Christmas.

Her heart clenched. She knew something about lonely holidays. "My ideal of Christmas was always the one in *Little Women,* where they all sacrificed to give to others and didn't need anything but each other to be happy." She'd reread that story every year at Christmastime.

"I remember it." His eyes met hers. "I'm sorry."

She knew he wasn't talking about Louisa May Alcott.

She bent over the playpen to hand Emilie a toy. "Actually my happiest Christmases have been the last few, once I figured out what it was we were celebrating."

"I wanted a bike for Christmas." Davey's voice startled her. She'd nearly forgotten the boy was there. "I asked for one last year, but my dad didn't have the money for it." He sat back on his heels. "It wasn't his fault, you know."

"I'm sure it wasn't," she said gently. Her heart hurt for him. "Maybe you'll be able to make enough money to buy a bike yourself."

Davey shot a glance at Mitch, then stared at the paintbrush in his hand. "Maybe." He didn't sound very optimistic.

Mitch reached over and touched the boy's shoulder lightly. Davey let the hand stay there for a moment, then pulled back.

Mitch looked at Anne, his smile a little crooked, and she knew he was as touched by the boy as she was. The sudden rapport, the sense of knowing what he was thinking—where had that come from? And what was she going to do about it?

"I'll start some lunch." She escaped to the other end of the kitchen, pulling open the refrigerator door to cool her face.

She'd never intended to let her guard down, never intended to see so deeply into someone's heart. She leaned her head against the edge of the refrigerator door. She and Mitch had begun to open up to each other in a way she hadn't expected. Now that he'd come so far into her life, how was she ever going to get him out again?

Anne pulled the mail from the box and checked it quickly. All for Kate. There was nothing that could be a response to the letter she'd sent to Marcy Brown's last known address.

Shivering a little in the cold wind, she closed the

mailbox and hurried back inside. Emilie was napping, and the house was too quiet. She stacked the mail on Kate's hall table. Something to do, she thought. She desperately needed something constructive to do.

Maybe Mitch's inquiries had gotten somewhere. But then, he'd have been in touch immediately.

She'd avoided him for the last few days. Maybe he'd been avoiding her, too, and for pretty much the same reason. After all, they both knew there couldn't be anything between them. The kind of closeness they'd experienced on Saturday could only be bittersweet in light of that. It was safer not to see much of each other, safer not to take the chance of wanting something she couldn't have.

She glanced at the phone. She'd called Helen in Philadelphia yesterday. Helen was the only one of her friends who knew the whole story, and so the only one she could talk to about it.

But Helen had been involved in dealing with a runaway in crisis, and Anne hadn't wanted to tie her up with her worries. So she'd just asked Helen to keep on praying about the situation.

"Always, child." Helen's voice was as warm as her heart. "You know I'm always praying for you and that dear baby God has given you. Trust Him."

Anne was trying so hard to trust.

If only she could think of something useful she could do. She'd tried Cassie again, but the woman hadn't remembered anything more. Then Anne had gotten a list from the pastor of everyone in the singles group. But no one seemed able to help. It was as if poor Tina hadn't made any impression at all in Bedford Creek. And Marcy Brown had disappeared, leaving no trace but a single Christmas card.

She walked restlessly back through the house to the kitchen and picked up the teakettle—

She stood still, kettle in hand, staring out the back window. Why was the shed door standing ajar?

She blinked, leaning a little closer to the window. Mitch had put the stepladder away in there on Saturday; she'd watched him do it. She'd seen him close and latch the door. Now it stood partially open.

Her heart began to thump. She should call the police, she should—

Now, wait a minute. The rational side of her brain kicked in. It was the middle of the afternoon. She was in Bedford Creek, not the big city. Why was she letting her imagination run away with her?

She grabbed her jacket from the hall closet and slipped out the back door. It would only take a moment to check. Probably the wind had blown the door open. Or maybe the latch had broken.

She crossed the wet grass, caught the door and pulled it wide, letting light flood the interior. It showed her the ladder, the lawn mower, the folding chair, an old croquet set.

And Davey Flagler, curled up under a wicker table, sound asleep.

"Davey?"

He woke instantly at the sound of her voice, and sat up so fast that his head brushed the table.

"Are you all right? What are you doing here?"

He slid out from under the table, face sullen. "Just sleeping, okay with you?"

"Seems like a cold place to sleep." Carefully, she thought. She had to handle him carefully. Whatever was wrong, she wouldn't get it by pushing. "Why don't you come in the house where it's warm?"

"Nah." He grabbed a small backpack he'd been using as a pillow. "Guess I'll get going now."

Anne didn't move from the doorway when he approached, and he glared up at her. "You going to let me out, or what?"

"Tell me what's going on, Davey." She gave him a level look. "You obviously should be in class, and here you are sleeping in Kate's shed. Is something wrong at school?"

He stared another moment, then his gaze slid away. His thin shoulders shrugged. "School's okay."

"Something wrong at home, then?" The little she knew about his family situation flashed through her mind.

"Look, I don't have to tell you anything. You're not my boss."

"No, but I'd like to be your friend. Come on, Davey. Tell me what's wrong. I won't tell anyone else, unless you say it's okay."

"Promise?" His tone was skeptical.

"I promise."

He stared down at the ground, his face troubled as he tried to put on a brave front. "We got evicted, that's what. Guess my dad was late with the rent again. Landlord threw us out."

His father must have been very late, if the landlord had gotten far enough in the legal process to evict them. She longed to touch the boy, but he was like a porcupine with all its quills standing on end.

"Is your dad out looking for another place?"

He shook his head.

"Then where is he?"

Davey didn't say anything, and a suspicion grew in her mind.

"Davey, you can trust me. Where's your father?"

He hesitated a moment longer. Then he looked up, and she thought she read fear behind the defiance in his eyes.

"He's gone, all right? He's gone, but he'll be back. I know he'll come back for me."

Oh, Lord, tell me what to do. My heart is breaking for this poor child, and I don't know how to help him.

Slowly, very slowly, she reached out to touch his shoulder. "Davey, I think you need some help with this one. You can't hide out in Kate's shed forever, you know."

"I don't want help!" He jerked away, fear leaping in his eyes. "You tell anyone, they'll maybe put me away."

"Nobody's going to put you away. I'm a lawyer, remember? I won't let them, okay?"

He studied her face for a moment, as if assessing the chance she was telling him the truth. Finally he nodded.

"Okay."

She let out the breath she'd been holding. "Maybe we ought to go down to the police station and—"

He went back a step, shaking his head. "No! I don't want to go there."

"What if Mitch comes here to talk to you? That's all—just talk."

His mouth set, and he stared down at his shoes. "All right," he said finally. "Long as all he wants to do is talk. He starts thinking about anything else, I'm outta here."

Luckily, Emilie was awake when they got into the house. Davey, fascinated, played with her, while Anne called Mitch and explained quickly.

He didn't bother asking for details or second-guessing her actions. "I'll be right there."

By the time Mitch arrived, they were all in the kitchen having a snack. Emilie gnawed on a biscuit while Davey wolfed down one sandwich after another.

"Hey, Davey." Mitch moved into the room easily, his voice low. He seemed to know without asking how skittish the boy was.

Davey eyed him suspiciously over the top of his

grilled-cheese sandwich. "You can't put me away. Anne already told me, and she's a lawyer. You can't put me away."

Mitch sank into a chair, reaching out to filch a quarter of a sandwich from Davey's plate. "Who said anything about putting you away?"

"Well, I'm just telling you." Some of the tension seemed to go out of him.

"You do need a place to stay, Davey," she pointed out. "You can't live in the shed."

"I can take care of myself. I'm almost eleven. I don't need anybody."

"You're not going to be put away, and you're not going to live in the shed." Mitch's voice was firm. "Way I see it, you just need a place to stay until your dad comes back. So, I figure the best thing is for you to move in with me."

Chapter Eleven

For an instant after the words were out of his mouth, Mitch couldn't believe he'd said them. What did he know about taking care of a kid, especially one with Davey's problems?

"Do you mean that?" Anne's gaze held his, warning him, maybe, that it was a bad thing to say if he didn't.

"I mean it." It felt right to him. The problem would probably be convincing the kid that it was right.

He glanced at Davey, who was looking at him with a startled, disbelieving expression. Was there a little hope in that look? He wasn't sure.

But he was sure of one thing. He'd begun to take some pride in the way the boy was shaping up, and he didn't intend to give up on him now.

Anne rested her hand lightly on Davey's shoulder. "Seems like a really good idea to me."

It was nice to see the approval in her eyes, but he wasn't doing it for that. He just couldn't let the kid slip through the cracks the way he almost had.

"What do you say, Davey? You willing to stay with me for a while?"

Davey stared at the tabletop, as if fascinated by it. "You don't need to. I'll be okay."

"Davey…" Carefully, now. He didn't want to scare the kid. "I know you're used to being pretty independent. But the law says you can't live on your own yet. So you've got to stay with someone. You have any relatives you'd rather be with?"

The boy shrugged. "Just my dad."

It had a familiar, lonely sound that reverberated in Mitch's heart. He didn't want to have to call Child Services on the kid. He wanted to work this out, somehow.

"Well, then, what do you say? I'm not that hard to get along with."

Davey stared at his hands. "Okay. I guess so." He looked up. "Just 'til my dad gets back. He'll come back for me."

"Sure he will." Mitch wouldn't dream of challenging the defiant note in the kid's voice. He'd have a look for Davey's father himself, but from what he'd seen, maybe the kid would be better off without him.

He wasn't about to sign on for the long haul, but he could do this much.

He could practically hear Anne's sigh of relief.

"You'll need to get approval as an emergency foster home from Child Services," she said. She was thinking like an attorney again. "I've been through that with Emilie, so I can help you out."

"Sounds good. I know the caseworkers. I don't think they'll raise any objections to Davey staying with me for the time being."

He'd always believed God had pulled him out of that quarry all those years ago for a reason. Maybe this was it.

Anne stood at the front window the next morning, watching as Davey, schoolbooks in hand, trudged down the street toward the school. She'd found it surprising how quickly and smoothly the question of Davey's custody had been settled. Maybe it was because Bedford Creek was a small town, or maybe because Mitch was the police chief. Nobody made waves about the situation.

He was now waiting in the doorway, maybe to be sure Davey headed in the right direction. Then Mitch went back inside, and the door closed. Apparently, he wasn't headed to work yet.

Anne stared thoughtfully at the house. If Mitch weren't at the office, he wouldn't see her heading into Ellie's gift shop. She bit her lip, torn by conflicting arguments.

So far she had nothing, absolutely nothing, to present at the adoption hearing about Emilie's father. Mitch's search had come up empty; everything Anne tried was a dead end.

But Ellie—Ellie might have had more to say if Mitch hadn't walked in on them. Anne could go back to see her. She could even bring up Tina's name and see if the woman remembered anything about her that might be a lead.

Ellie was too bright to interpret a second visit as something casual. She'd know this was important to Anne. She'd be curious; she might talk about it.

But the clock was ticking. Maybe the time had passed for the caution she'd agreed to when she'd come to Bedford Creek. If there was the faintest possibility Ellie had answers, Anne had to go after them.

Kate, who'd returned the previous evening, leaped at the chance to watch Emilie when Anne said she wanted to go out. Anne hurried to the car. It would be faster to drive, with less chance of running into Mitch coming or going and forcing her to explain why she was talking to Ellie again.

A parking space in front of the shop, no other customers… She couldn't imagine why Ellie bothered to open until tourist season, but she was grateful for it.

Ellie raised her eyebrows when she walked up to the counter. "Are you interested in another wreath?"

"Not exactly." How much did Ellie guess of her motives? "We didn't really have a chance to finish our conversation the other day."

Ellie shrugged, dark eyes wary. "We were interrupted, remember?"

"Yes, well, I thought we might talk about it a little more." The woman was so cautious, it was difficult to read her.

Ellie stared at her for a long moment, then leaned against the counter. "Did you have any luck with the address I gave you?"

"Marcy had moved, and there wasn't a phone listing for her. I sent a letter, hoping it would be forwarded, but I haven't heard anything yet." And maybe she never would.

"What else do you want? I don't know any other way to find Marcy. She's not good about keeping in touch, and we weren't best friends or anything."

"I wondered..." This was the tricky part, and there didn't seem to be any casual way to bring it up. "I wondered if you remembered another friend of hers—Tina Mallory."

Ellie stared at her, eyes unreadable. Then she shrugged again. "I remember her. I never knew her very well, though. Are you trying to find her, too?"

Obviously she found Anne's interest suspicious, to say the least. "No. Tina was the mutual friend I mentioned. The one who died a few months ago."

"That young girl?" Ellie's reaction was much the

same as Cassie's had been. "That's hard to believe. What happened to her?"

"She had a heart problem that had never been diagnosed." Anne felt as if she were using Tina's death to gain the woman's cooperation. "I know she and Marcy were good friends, and I thought Marcy ought to be told, but I haven't been able to locate her."

Ellie shook her head. "Wish I could help, but I don't know any other way to find her."

"Maybe you remember other friends Tina made when she lived here." Surely she remembered something helpful. "I'd like to get in touch with them, too."

"I can't think of any." Ellie frowned. "She was a dreamy kid, kept pretty much to herself. I never got to know her very well."

"What about boyfriends?" The opportunity was slipping through her fingers, dissolving away into mist like every other lead to Emilie's father.

"Boyfriends?" Ellie looked at her with an expression Anne couldn't interpret.

"Yes, boyfriends." Maybe she didn't sound as pushy as she feared she did. "She was a young girl. She must have gone out with someone while she was here."

"Funny you should ask me about that." Ellie picked up one of the dried-flower arrangements on the counter, tweaking it as if to keep her hands busy.

"What's funny about it?"

"Funny because you're such good friends with Mitch Donovan."

"What do you mean?" A heavy weight seemed to press down on her, as if she knew the answer before the woman spoke.

Ellie twisted a flower into place, then looked at her. "I thought he was the man Tina dated."

Pain ricocheted through her. It carried a clear message. She'd gotten far too involved with Mitch Donovan—been far too willing to believe him.

She cleared her throat, trying not to let her voice or her face express any emotion at all. "What makes you think that?"

Ellie frowned, dark braids flapping as she shook her head. "Not sure, really."

Anne had to have more than this. "Did you see them together?"

"No...no, I don't believe I ever did. Unless maybe it was at the café. Tina worked there, you know."

"Yes, I know. But you must have some reason for thinking they went out besides seeing Tina wait on him."

Or did she? Anne wondered. Sometimes body language between two people told you all you needed to know about their relationship. Her stomach knotted at the thought.

"Maybe it was something Tina said. Or Marcy said." Her face brightened. "Yes, that's it. It was something Marcy said."

Anne's heart pounded loudly enough for her to hear, but she'd keep her voice level in spite of it. "What did Marcy say?"

"Well, I don't remember exactly."

She gripped the counter, holding back the need to shake the truth out of the woman. "What *do* you remember?"

"Seems to me…" She paused, head cocked as if listening to voices in the past. "I know what it was. Marcy said Tina was crazy about the chief. 'Head over heels in love with him'—that's what she said."

Head over heels in love. Anne wanted to grapple with Ellie's revelation, to assess it the way she would any piece of evidence in a case, but she couldn't seem to make her mind work that way. Ellie's words had blown a gigantic hole through her heart.

This is crazy. How could her instincts possibly be so far off the mark? She thought she knew Mitch. How could the person who helped her when she was sick, who took in young Davey, possibly have been lying to her all along?

She couldn't reconcile the two images of Mitch. They just didn't fit.

She'd begun to trust him. That was what drove the hurt deep into her heart. She didn't rely on people easily, thanks to her parents' example, but she'd begun to count on Mitch. How could she possibly be so wrong?

There was only one thing to do, one way to cope with this. She'd have to confront Mitch and find out the truth, Anne decided as she left Ellie's shop and got into her car.

But her courage left her when she reached Mitch's house. What was she going to say? How could she believe him?

She had to confront him with it, that was all. Nothing would be more unfair than to condemn him on the basis of a rumor. No matter how difficult, she had to face him. She rang the bell.

She had rung it a second time before she heard answering footsteps in the hall beyond.

"All right, all right." The masculine grumble sounded annoyed. "I'm coming." The door swung open.

"Anne." A quick smile lit his eyes. "Come in." He gestured with the hand that didn't hold the overflowing laundry basket. "I'm getting caught up on a few things before I go to the station."

She followed him into the hallway.

"We picked up Davey's clothes last night. Poor kid doesn't have much, and what he does have needed to be washed." He set the basket down. "I thought I'd..."

He stopped suddenly, his dark brown eyes focusing on her face. He went still, his gaze probing as if he could see into her heart.

"What is it? What's wrong?"

"I... " She opened her mouth, then closed it again. This was so difficult. The home he'd created surrounded her, warm and welcoming. It didn't seem the right place for the accusation she had to make. And she couldn't fool herself, any more than she could fool him. It *was* an accusation.

"Tell me." He reached toward her, but stopped before his fingers touched her arm.

Maybe she was putting out warning signals, she thought.

"What's going on?" he pressed.

"I talked to Ellie this morning." *Just get it out, any way you can.* "I asked her about Tina. She remembered something."

His face stiffened. "It can't have been anything good."

"Why do you say that?"

"Because you look ready for a fight, Counselor."

If he wanted the facts, he was going to get them. "Ellie remembered Marcy talking about Tina. And you."

"There was no Tina and me." He narrowed his eyes. "No matter what Ellie says."

"Ellie wasn't making any accusations." Her voice grew stronger as the woman's words rang in her mind. "She was just repeating what Marcy said."

"And that was…?"

"That Tina was crazy about you. 'Head over heels in love'—that's what she said."

He looked…astonished. That was the only word for it. "Ellie said that? I knew she didn't like me, but I didn't think she'd make up something about me."

"She wasn't. At least, I don't think she was doing anything other than repeating what Marcy had said to her."

"Hearsay, Counselor?"

She stiffened. "We're not in a court of law. I'm trying to find the truth. The two things don't always go together."

"No, I guess not." He took a step toward her. "But I thought we were beginning to trust each other."

She winced at the pain in his voice. That had to be genuine, didn't it?

"I just…I just don't know."

"We're back at the same old impasse then, aren't we." His mouth hardened. "All I can say is that I barely knew the girl. If she had feelings for me, I wasn't aware of it. I certainly never dated her."

"Then why?" Her voice threatened to break. "Why would she say those things?"

She flung out her hands, and the question seemed to vibrate in the air between them.

"I don't know." His voice was heavy, final. "I guess there's nothing else to say."

She swallowed hard. "I guess there isn't. When the DNA results come—"

"When the DNA results come, you'll know I'm

telling the truth. I wish you could trust me until then, but it's pretty clear you can't.''

Everything in her cried out to believe him. But she couldn't. She could only shake her head and walk away.

Mitch tried to ignore the emotions that surged through him. It didn't work. They pounded at him. Anger, pain, disappointment. He'd thought... *What* had he thought? That she'd begun to care for him? That she returned the caring he'd tried so hard not to admit?

He couldn't deny it now. He looked bleakly at it. He cared for her. And she didn't trust him. That was it, bottom line. She didn't trust him.

Just like his father. Nobody'd trusted Ken Donovan, with good reason. He'd betrayed everyone who'd made that mistake—every friend, every employer. Everyone who'd given him a chance to make something of himself.

And then he'd betrayed his family. To Mitch, looking at that was like looking into a black hole. Worse, it was a hole that threatened to suck him in.

The doorbell rang. Anne? Impossible.

But he crossed the hall in a few long strides, grabbed the knob and flung the door open. And looked into the face of his brother.

''Link.''

''Hey, big brother.'' Link slouched through the door without waiting for an invitation. He dropped an overloaded duffel bag on the floor and turned to Mitch. "Don't look so glad to see me."

In spite of everything that experience had taught him to expect from Link, he couldn't help a surge of affection. Link, looking at him with that boyish grin, hair falling in his eyes, was for a moment the little brother he'd tried to teach and protect.

He held out his hand. "It's been a long time."

Link gripped his hand briefly. "Can't say it looks like much has changed in Bedford Creek while I've been gone."

"Don't suppose it has." Be careful. He couldn't let Link in on the biggest change in Bedford Creek. The one in the house right across the street. Link wouldn't be any support. In fact, he'd probably enjoy seeing Mitch embarrassed.

"Small town attitudes, small town minds." The familiar mocking note came into Link's voice. "How do you stand it?"

"I'm happy here. Some people wouldn't be." He snapped the words.

"Happy? How can you be happy knowing everyone in this town is looking down at you?"

"Nobody looks down at me." His temper flared. That was Link, pushing the familiar buttons. "Not anymore."

"Yeah, right." Contempt saturated the words. "You're the police chief now. That just means they'll use you to clean up their messes. But don't make the mistake of thinking they have any respect for you.''

''You'd know a lot about that, wouldn't you? You don't have any respect for anyone or anything.''

They were back to the old arguments, the ones they never seemed to get past.

Link shrugged. ''I just look at the world a little differently from the way you do. Realistically. Nobody's going to give you a break, so don't expect it, and you won't be disappointed.''

Like Anne, who didn't trust him, Mitch thought. He stared bleakly at his brother, wondering how, in a few short moments, Link had managed to zero in on his pain.

Chapter Twelve

Anne looked out the front window the next morning for what must have been the twentieth time. The police car still sat in the driveway, so Mitch hadn't left yet. Also for the twentieth time, she longed to run across the street, to tell him she believed in him. DNA results or not, she believed in him.

But she couldn't do it. Each time she thought she was ready to take that step, something held her back.

When she thought of the pain in Mitch's eyes the day before, she wanted to do whatever it would take to wipe it away.

Then the doubts crept in, poisoning her thoughts. What if she was wrong? What if Ellie's presumption was true? What if Mitch really had been the man in Tina's life?

Why can't I know, Lord? Why can't I know the truth, and then I could trust him?

No calmness came to still the tumult inside her. No answer presented itself, fully formed, in her mind. She didn't know, she just didn't know.

She heard the steps creak outside and turned back to the window in time to see the mail carrier going down. Kate was busy in the back of the house; Emilie safely napping upstairs She might as well bring the mail in.

Anne carried a fat bundle inside and began to sort it on the hall table. Most of it was for Kate, of course, but—

She stared at the envelope with McKay Laboratories on the return address, and her heart started to hammer uncomfortably.

It was here. The DNA report was here, a week earlier than she'd hoped. When she'd called the lab to give them her address in Bedford Creek, she'd been told they were backed up with tests.

"Anne? Is something wrong?"

She'd been so preoccupied that she hadn't heard Kate come in from the kitchen. The elderly woman was drying her hands on a tea towel, looking curiously at her.

"No, no, nothing." Her face must betray that as a lie. "I'm fine. Excuse me."

Clutching the envelope, she hurried up the stairs. Kate would think her rude, but she just couldn't help it. She had to get away from the woman's curious eyes while she held Emilie's fate in her hands.

She slipped into the sitting room quietly and sank

into the nearest chair. It was here, and now that it was, she could hardly bear to open it. She wanted to know; she was afraid to know.

Help me, Lord. Please help me. I'm afraid.

Suddenly the conviction she'd been seeking filled her, taking her breath away. The certainty pooled inside her, deep and sure. It wasn't Mitch. Whoever it was, it wasn't Mitch.

She opened the envelope and pulled out the results. They confirmed what she already knew. Mitch Donovan hadn't fathered Tina's child.

Thank you, Lord. Thank you.

She had to tell him. She folded the envelope and stuck it in her pocket. She had to tell him, now.

Kate stood in the hallway, glancing through a catalog. She looked up as Anne came down the stairs.

"I don't know why they keep sending me these things. I never order anything from them." Her gaze was keen on Anne's face, but clearly she wouldn't intrude.

Anne swallowed hard. She'd like to confide in Kate, but she couldn't. "I need to speak to Mitch for a moment, and Emilie's napping. Would you mind…?"

"Of course not." Kate's response was immediate. "You go on. Take as long as you want."

She'd reached Mitch's door before the thought occurred to her that he might be angry. He might well say, "I told you so."

Well, he deserved to be able to say it, and she

had to give him that chance. She knocked at the door.

Mitch pulled it open, his gaze both surprised and wary when he saw her. "Anne."

"May I come in?"

"Of course." He stepped back, his expression giving nothing away.

She walked in, trying to find the right words. Funny, she'd felt just that way the first time she'd seen him. Apprehensive, tense, struggling to find the right words. Maybe there weren't any.

She swung toward him and held out the envelope. He took it automatically, staring from it to her with a frowning intensity.

"It came." She took a breath. "I want you to know this. I don't see any reason why you should believe it, but it's true. Before I opened the envelope, I knew what it would say. I knew it wasn't you."

He flicked at the opened envelope flap with his finger. "I see you still had to look."

All right, she deserved that. "Yes, I guess I did."

He nodded, his face expressionless. Then he handed the envelope back.

"Aren't you going to look at it?"

He lifted an eyebrow. "Why? I know what it says."

She turned away from that searching gaze. "I wish..." Her cheeks grew warm. "I wish things could have been different. I'm sorry I put you through this. Maybe I never should have come to Bedford Creek.''

He took a step closer, not touching her, but close enough that she could feel the heat of his body. "If you'd never come, I'd never have met you.''

She tried to smile. "I would think you'd consider that an advantage.''

He shook his head. "I'll trade the suspicion for the chance to know you any day of the week.''

For a moment her eyes met his. The barriers he usually put up were gone, and she seemed able to see right into his soul. To see the integrity. He wasn't a man who hid his weaknesses behind a façade. The only thing hiding behind his mask was strength.

He reached out to touch her cheek. His palm was warm and strong against her skin. The feel of him seemed to spread out from his fingers, coursing along her nerve endings, warming her all the way through.

"Mitch.'' She barely breathed his name.

He slid his hand down her neck, leaving longing in its wake. He grasped her shoulder and drew her toward him.

It was all right now. He hadn't been involved with Tina; he wasn't lying to her. She could trust him. She could let herself care about him. She leaned toward him, expecting to feel his lips on hers.

Instead he held her close, his cheek against hers.

"Will you tell me something?" His voice was soft, a whisper in her ear.

"Tell you what?" How she could think clearly enough to tell him anything, she couldn't imagine. Her mind seemed totally involved in the feel of his cheek was against hers, how strong his muscles were under her hand, how the two of them fit together perfectly.

"Tell me why it's so hard for you to trust."

The words brought her back…back to a world where explanations had to be made, where people had a right to know things, no matter how painful.

She met his eyes. "Are you sure you want to know?"

Mitch watched the play of emotion on her face. She'd come so far into his life in such a short time and now he couldn't imagine doing without her.

"I think I already know some of this. It has to do with your parents, doesn't it?"

He could feel the resistance in her. She didn't want to tell him this. The muscles in her neck worked, as if she had swallowed something unpalatable.

"Poor little rich girl." Her voice mocked herself. "That's what it sounds like, so I don't talk about it."

"You can talk about it to me." He led her to the sofa, sat down next to her. "I want to understand."

He managed a smile. "After all, you know the worst about me, don't you?"

She stared down at her hands, still resisting, still holding back. Then she looked up at him, her eyes defiant. "My parents never hit me. They never mistreated me. I had everything I needed."

He rested his hand on the nape of her neck, feeling the tension there. "You couldn't have had everything you needed, or you wouldn't feel the way you do."

Anne stiffened. "There's nothing wrong with the way I feel. I just…"

"You just can't rely on anyone."

"Well, maybe I can't. Maybe people aren't very reliable."

"Some aren't." He met her look steadily. "But some are."

"I guess I have trouble telling the difference. After all, I was married to someone who recreated the same pattern. That wasn't smart, was it?"

Her anger was still there, but he recognized it for the defense it was. If they were ever going to get past this, he had to get her to level with him.

"I think I can almost fill in the blanks." It could be that throwing it right at her was the only way. "Your parents provided you with every material thing you needed. They just neglected the little things—love, attention, support."

"They probably thought they were doing the right

things for me. I should have been stronger. I should have been able…''

''What? To tell them how to be parents?'' Anger licked along his veins, at two selfish people he'd never known. ''They had a beautiful child, and they never bothered to let her know just how precious she was.''

''You don't know that.''

She tried to smile, but it was a pitiful effort that wrung his heart. He could feel the pride that had kept her silent slipping away.

''I used to think maybe I wasn't pretty enough, or special enough, or what they wanted.'' She shook her head. ''I used to think if only I'd been a boy, it would have been different. My father always wanted a son.''

He slid his hand comfortingly down the long sweet curve of her back. ''Used to think?''

She glanced at him, and he saw the tears that sparkled on the verge of spilling over. ''Then I met my friend, Helen. And through Helen, I found out I had another Friend. One who considered me precious, even if my parents hadn't.''

He nodded. ''I thought it was something like that. When I saw the dedication in your Bible.''

Her blinding smile broke through the tears that had gathered. ''First it was Helen, introducing me to the Lord. And then God brought me Emilie. Once I had a child, I realized how wrong they'd been. Emilie opened me up to a whole new dimension in my life. I could never ignore her the way they ignored me.''

The smile hurt his heart. He wanted her to smile that way for him. To light up because he was part of her life, too.

''She means everything to you.''

''She means—'' Her voice choked a little. ''If I have Emilie to love, none of the rest of it matters. If I don't…''

She stopped, and he saw the pain that filled her eyes. Pain and fear.

''What if I lose her? What if I go into that hearing with nothing, and the court decides to put her into a foster home? It could happen. I've seen it happen.''

''It's not going to happen. Not to you and Emilie.''

He wanted to wipe the fear away, banish it for good. Why couldn't he do that one thing for her? *Assist, protect, defend.* He wasn't doing a very good job of any of those for Anne.

''You don't know that.'' Her hands clenched. ''No one knows.''

''Don't.'' He drew her close against him, wanting only to comfort her. ''Don't torture yourself like this.''

''I can't help it.'' She turned her face into his chest, and he felt her ragged breath on his skin through the thin cotton of his shirt.

''It's going to be all right.'' He cradled her face

between his palms so he could see her eyes, will her to believe him. "You've got to hold on to that."

Her gaze locked with his, and as her eyes darkened, all the breath seemed to go out of him. Her lips were a scant inch from his, and he longed to close the gap, to taste her mouth, wrap his arms around her and not let go. But how could he? What she needed from him was comfort now.

Then she lifted her mouth to his, and all his rational thought exploded into fragments. He drew her closer, the blood pounding through his veins. Her mouth was warm and sweet, and the two of them fit together as if they'd been made for each other.

This was right. It had to be.

"Well, well—"

The voice was like a splash of icy water in Mitch's face.

"—looks like my big brother has company."

Mitch let her go so suddenly that for an instant Anne was totally disoriented. She had to force herself out of a world that had included no one but her and Mitch. Someone else had come in. What was a stranger doing in Mitch's house?

Except that it wasn't a stranger. Mitch had said his name. *Link.* This had to be the brother—the one Mitch didn't want to talk about.

"Mitch, aren't you going to introduce me to your friend?" He crossed toward them from the hall, his walk an easy slouch as different as possible from Mitch's military bearing.

Mitch didn't speak, and his silence made her nervous. She held out her hand.

"I'm Anne Morden." She bit back any further explanation. To say anything more would show her embarrassment, would imply she had some reason to feel embarrassed.

Link took her hand, holding it a bit longer than was necessary. "Link Donovan. Mitch's little brother."

He was slighter than Mitch, not quite as tall or as broad. But the same dark-brown hair fell on his forehead, longer and more unruly than Mitch's military cut, and the same chocolate-brown eyes assessed her.

"Link is here for a visit. A brief one." Mitch seemed to make an effort to rouse himself from his silence.

"He works out west."

"Sometimes." Link eyed him. "Sometimes my travels bring me back to Pennsylvania, and good old Bedford Creek. My big brother would rather I stayed out west."

"I didn't say that." Mitch grated the words.

Anne looked at him. Mitch had the closed, barricaded look he'd worn the first time she met him. She thought she sensed anger seething underneath, but he obviously didn't intend to let it out.

"Close enough." Link shrugged. "But here I am

back again, like the proverbial bad penny. And Mitch still wishes I'd go away."

That was clearly an appropriate time for Mitch to protest that he didn't want to be rid of his brother, Anne thought. But he didn't. He just gave Link that daunting stare.

She, at least, would have found it daunting. But Link seemed unaffected.

He shrugged. "Well, guess I'll let you get back to…whatever it was you were doing."

He sauntered back out again, and in a moment she heard the front door slam.

She'd opened her mouth to say some conventional words, but Link had gotten out the door before she could muster them.

Mitch shot off the couch. He strode to the window and looked out, as if assuring himself that Link was gone. "Sorry. Link just showed up yesterday. He does that."

"Not very often, it seems." She tread warily, not sure of his feelings.

"It's been two years," Mitch said. "I could see your mind working when you looked at him. You were wondering if he could be Emilie's father."

"I suppose I was." That should hardly surprise him, under the circumstances. "I wonder that about every man I meet in Bedford Creek."

"You don't need to wonder about Link." His voice was harsh. "I know exactly when he was here last. Two years ago next month, right at Easter.

Wanting me to bail him out of trouble again, like he always does.''

His anger seemed all out of proportion, and she felt her way, unsure what was driving it. Or what she could do to defuse it.

''And did you help him?''

Mitch's frown darkened. ''I lent him money again. Although I don't think *lend* is the right word, since he's never repaid a cent. And then I told him it was the last time. That he'd better find someone else to get him out of trouble, because I wouldn't do it again.''

Thoughts tumbled through her mind, most of which were probably better not expressed. ''I see.'' But she didn't.

''I never figured I'd say that about my own brother. When we were kids, I used to think we'd always be best friends.''

He went silent, and she tried to find the words that would get him talking again.

''I always dreamed of having a brother or sister,'' she began. ''I imagined it would be the best thing, to have someone to share things with.''

''There wasn't much to share at our house.'' His mouth became a thin line. ''Except maybe a slap or two when our father had had too much to drink.''

''You tried to protect your brother.'' She knew that much without asking. It was in his nature.

''I tried. But Link figured out early how to talk

his way out of trouble. And he did it even if that meant he blamed me.''

Anne could sense the pain he'd felt at his brother's betrayal. ''Mitch, you can't still hold him responsible for that. Any kid would—''

He swung toward her. ''I don't blame him for that.'' The words shot toward her, loud in the quiet room. ''I blame him because he's turned out just like our father. I can't understand that, and I don't think I ever will.''

The pain came through in his words so clearly that it pierced her heart. She suddenly saw a younger Mitch, trying to protect his brother and having that protection thrown back in his face.

''No.'' She said it softly. ''I guess I wouldn't, either.''

For a moment he didn't respond. Then his head jerked in the briefest of nods.

Let me in. Please don't shut me out. ''Have you been in touch with him at all since that last time?''

''No. I didn't expect to hear from him. He'd stay away until he thought I had time to get over it. Until he thought he could hit me up for money again.''

''Maybe he's changed. Maybe he's done some growing up since then.''

He shook his head. ''Look, there's no point in rehashing this. Link is the way he is, and I don't figure I'm ever going to change him. I'm just sorry he came in when he did.''

''Because we were kissing?'' She smiled, inviting

him to see the humor in it. "That's not so bad, is it?"

"You don't understand." His face refused to relax. "Link would like nothing better than to embarrass me."

She raised her eyebrows. "Why is it embarrassing to be caught kissing someone? You're not hiding a wife in the closet, are you?"

He shook his head stubbornly. "It's not funny. You don't know what he's like."

"I know what you're like." She closed the space between them, putting her hand on his arm. It was like a bar of iron. "Link doesn't matter to me, except for the way he affects you."

"I shouldn't have kissed you, knowing he could walk in at any minute. I should have had more sense."

Her patience abruptly ran out. She was trying to be reasonable, trying to be on his side, and he just wouldn't let her. "If that's the way you feel about it, maybe you shouldn't have kissed me at all." She snatched her jacket from the chair. "I think I'd better go."

He didn't try to stop her.

Chapter Thirteen

〜

"Finish up that homework before you watch television." Mitch leaned over the history book and notebook Davey had spread out on the kitchen table. "Mrs. Prentice said you're behind in your assignments."

Davey gave him a rebellious look. He picked up the yellow pencil with an elaborate sigh.

At least there was one person in his life who wasn't arguing with him. Mitch picked up the dish towel and started drying the silverware from dinner. Davey might be unhappy about having someone keep an eye on him while he did homework, but maybe at some level he understood Mitch was doing it because he cared. Mitch hoped so, anyway.

Understanding didn't extend to other people in his life. Anne didn't understand why he felt the way he did about his brother. As for Link... Who knew what Link understood? How to get his own way— that was all that had ever mattered to him. He didn't care about anything else.

He tossed a handful of spoons into the drawer. Link's return had upset too much. He should be with Anne right now, helping her, mapping out a plan for the adoption hearing. Instead she was so angry she'd probably slam the door in his face if he went over there.

He couldn't blame her for that. He hadn't intended it, but to her it had probably sounded as if he were ashamed of kissing her. Of caring about her.

I didn't mean it. He tried saying the words in his mind, tried imagining what her response would be.

Nothing encouraging appeared. Instead, he could only see her face the way it had looked earlier— angry, hurt, disappointed.

"You two look busy." Link's tone made it clear he didn't mean that as a compliment.

Mitch turned toward the doorway. Link's hair was wet from the shower, his shirt and pants freshly pressed.

"Going somewhere?"

"You're not wishing me gone, are you, big brother?"

Aware of Davey's dark eyes watching them, Mitch shook his head. "I already said you were welcome." *As long as you don't cause trouble.* "I just wondered where you were off to."

Link swung a leather jacket around his shoulders. "Going to meet up with some of the guys. It'll be just like old times."

"Not too much like old times, I hope." Link had run with a rough crowd in high school, and Mitch had no desire to have to arrest his own brother.

"You never did think much of my friends." A defensive note crept into Link's voice.

Mitch gave him a level look. "I think of them as little as possible. You'd be better off if you did the same."

"Hey, you've got your friends, and I've got mine. Can't say I ever cared for yours, but maybe your taste is improving. Your Anne's a cut above most of the local talent. You seeing her tonight?"

He should be. "No."

"Too bad." Link didn't sound sorry. "Maybe you scared her off. Maybe she'd like to try out a different Donovan brother."

The plate he was holding clattered into the dish drainer, and Mitch took a step toward his brother. "You leave her out of this, you hear?"

Link lifted a mocking eyebrow. "Little bit of a sore spot there? Hey, don't worry. She's not my type, anyway." He turned away. "Expect me when you see me."

Mitch counted to ten, then made it twenty. Nobody could make him madder than Link could. Maybe that was because nobody knew his trigger spots quite so well. Or enjoyed pushing them quite as much.

He turned back to the table, to discover Davey was gone. The history book still lay there, and the notebook was pristine. If any homework had been done, there was no sign of it.

Fuming, he went in search of the boy. He found him in the living room, parked in front of the television. Mitch snapped off the set in the middle of a car chase, earning a glare from Davey.

"Hey! I was watching that."

"How about your homework?"

"Done." Davey's tone was airy. "All done."

Mitch held out the text and notebook. "Show me. You were supposed to write the answers to ten questions. Show me."

"Listen, I know all that stuff. I don't need to write it down."

"If you knew all that stuff, you wouldn't be getting a *D* in history."

"It's dumb, anyway." Davey glared at him. "I'll bet you never did your homework. I'll bet your brother never did. So why do I have to?"

"Because I said so!" There were a lot better reasons than that, but at the moment his fuse was so short that he couldn't think of any. He tossed the book at Davey. "Get up to your room, and don't come out until the work is finished. And don't count on watching TV again any time soon."

"You're not my boss!" Davey let the book fall

to the floor. "I don't have to do what you say. When my father comes back—"

"If your father comes back, you can argue with him. Until then, you'll live by my rules." He scooped the book off the floor and shoved it into Davey's hands. "Now go upstairs and get started."

Davey glared at him for another moment. Then he turned and stamped up the stairs, each footstep making its own protest. The door to his bedroom slammed shut.

Mitch held on to the conviction that he was right for about another minute-and-a-half. Then his anger cooled and the truth seeped in. He'd just blown up at Davey because he was angry with Link. To say nothing of being angry with himself.

Oh, he was right: the kid had to do his homework. But Mitch was the grown-up in the equation. He shouldn't have lost his temper. He certainly shouldn't have said anything about Davey's father.

He glanced uncertainly toward the stairs. Should he go up and apologize? Or say something about the boy's father? But the man seemed to have done an excellent job of disappearing.

He could have stood some impartial advice. If he hadn't made Anne thoroughly disgusted with him, he could have asked her. She and Davey seemed to have connected. But that door was closed until he managed to make amends.

Maybe the best thing was to leave the kid alone for a bit. He glanced at his watch. He'd give Davey an hour, then see how he was getting along. If he hadn't done the questions by then, maybe he could use some help. Then they could have a snack and watch something on television together, the way he'd always imagined families did.

Mitch sat down with the newspaper and tried to concentrate on the printed words. Unfortunately, too many things kept intruding. Was he doing the right thing for Davey? What was he going to do about Link? And most of all, how could he make things right with Anne?

Her face seemed to form against the black-and-white page, angry and hurt. The two of them had been closer than they'd ever been this afternoon. They'd reached a new level of understanding and trust, quite apart from the kiss that had shaken him as he'd never been shaken in his life.

And then it had all fallen apart.

Finally he put the paper down and looked at his watch: forty-five minutes. Good enough. He'd go fix things with Davey. It would be practice for trying to fix things with Anne.

He went up the steps quickly, forming the words in his mind. No indication that he was backing down on the homework issue, just a friendly offer to help—that was the right tone to take.

He tapped lightly on the door, then opened it. "Davey?"

He was talking to an empty room. The history

book lay on the crumpled bed, and the window stood open to the cold night air. Davey was gone.

Anne put a light blanket over Emilie, tucking it around the sleeping baby. Emilie sprawled on her back, rosy face turned slightly to the side, hands outstretched. The pose spoke of perfect trust, perfect confidence. In Emilie's view of the world, everything was secure.

A lump formed in Anne's throat. Emilie didn't know it, but things weren't as secure as all that. Anne was the only person standing between her and an uncertain future. She'd never before felt so alone.

For a few brief moments that afternoon she'd begun to think life didn't have to be this way. She'd started to believe she really could have the kind of relationship she'd always thought was a mirage— one based on trust and openness. Something very good had begun between her and Mitch.

And then Mitch let his feelings about his brother spoil everything. Why couldn't he talk to her about it? He'd been so determined to hold everything inside, so irrationally angry. She didn't understand, and she probably never would.

The doorbell rang, suddenly and persistently, breaking the stillness in the old house. Startled, she closed the door to the bedroom gently, then went out into the hallway. She leaned over the stairs. What on earth was going on?

She saw Kate hurry toward the door. If something

was wrong, she shouldn't let Kate face it alone. She started down the steps as the older woman unlocked the door and pulled it open.

Mitch erupted into the hallway. "Have you seen Davey?"

"No, not today." Kate ushered Mitch in and closed the door. "Why?"

Heart pounding, Anne hurried down the rest of the stairs. Mitch wouldn't look like that unless something had happened.

"Mitch?"

He looked over Kate's head toward Anne. "It's Davey. He's run away."

She barely registered Kate's exclamations of dismay. She was too occupied with the message Mitch's dark eyes were sending her.

Help. For the first time in their relationship, he wanted—needed—her help.

"What can we do?" Knowing why the boy had run could wait. Finding him—that was the important thing.

"I thought maybe he'd come over here." He glanced at Kate.

"We haven't seen hide nor hair of him." Kate clasped her hands in front of her. "Poor child. It's getting cold out, too. He shouldn't be out there in the cold and the dark. If he goes into the woods—"

"What do you want us to do?" she asked again. Mitch needed their help, not Kate's woeful predictions.

He shook his head. "Not much you can do if he hasn't come here. I'll get some people together and start a search."

"Maybe he'll come back on his own. Once he cools off, I mean."

"I did that a time or two." A muscle twitched in Mitch's jaw. "But I was a teenager then, not a ten-year-old. And it's supposed to drop below freezing tonight. I don't think it's safe to wait."

"No." She shivered, thinking of the lonely mountainous woods that surrounded Bedford Creek. "Let me get a coat. I'll help look."

"You don't know the area well enough." His rejection seemed automatic, but she wasn't going to be left behind to worry.

"I'm another pair of eyes. I can go with someone who does know." *Like you.*

Mitch gave a curt nod, obviously too intent on the search to argue.

"I'll watch the baby." Kate seemed glad to have something constructive to do. "I'll put the outside lights on, so he'll know someone's home if he wants to come here. And I'll start the prayer chain, if that's all right with you."

Mitch nodded. He looked at Anne. "Ready?"

"Right away." She grabbed her jacket from the coat tree.

"Let's get down to the station. I'll call the search team out from there."

She hurried after him down the steps, his anxiety

palpable, pulling her along. *Hurry, hurry.* The cold wind, whistling down the mountain, made her thrust her hands into her pockets.

"He'll be all right." She said it to Mitch's back. "We'll find him."

He yanked open the cruiser door, and she slid into the passenger seat. When he got in beside her, his face was taut in the glare that spilled from the dome light.

"I hope so. Looks like I was the wrong choice for the boy."

She shook her head. "If you made a mistake, you can fix it. The important thing now is to find him."

For a moment longer he stared at her. Then he nodded, and his usual stoic mask seemed to fall into place.

"Right." He clasped her hand for an instant. "Thanks."

He started the police car, and it lurched forward.

She peered out the side window as the car spun around the corner. Dark, too dark to see much. She leaned her forehead against the window, hoping against hope that Davey would spring suddenly into view, safe and sound.

But he didn't.

Please, Lord. She stared out into the darkness. *Please, Lord. Be with us and guide our search. And be with that poor lost child.*

She hugged herself, shaking a little. A lost child.

At the moment it seemed they were all lost children, in one way or another.

"Shall we have a moment of prayer before we start?" Pastor Richie stepped to the front of the group of searchers who'd gathered at the station.

Anne could sense the urgency seething in Mitch, but he nodded. She clasped her hands in prayer. They needed all the help they could get. Twenty searchers, armed with powerful flashlights, looked like a lot, especially when coupled with those who were already cruising the streets in cars. But it probably wasn't enough—not when they were looking for one small boy in the dark.

Pastor Richie lifted his hands. "Loving Father, we come to You in desperate need. One of Your children is lost. Guide our search, that we may restore him to safety. We know You're watching each of us as a loving father tends his children. We put our search in Your strong hands. In Christ's name we pray, Amen."

Please, Lord.

She saw Mitch's hands flex, as if he were trying to relieve the tension. Again she felt the urgency that drove him.

"Okay," he said. "You have your assignments. Everybody know what to do?"

She nodded with the rest. It had already been decided she'd go with Mitch, giving him another pair of eyes to search the blocks around his house.

"All right. Let's go find him."

The crowd scattered quickly.

Mitch slid into the car and turned the key in the ignition before she even got the door closed. "I don't think he'll have gone far."

The streetlights they passed first illuminated his face, then cast it in shadow.

She clasped her hands. "What if he has some destination in mind?"

He sent her a sharp glance. "What do you mean? What destination?"

She didn't want to say this, but she had to. "Maybe he wants to find his father."

"He's said he doesn't know where he is. Anyway..." His voice trailed off.

She thought she could fill in the blanks. Mitch wouldn't have gone after his own father, or at least that's what he told himself now. So he didn't want to believe it of Davey, either.

Help him, Lord, please. This is really hurting him. It reminds him too much of his own past.

Mitch pulled to the curb at the end of the block and grabbed a flashlight. "Look, we've got to make some assumptions to go on. I don't think he's on a wild-goose chase after his dad, but if he is, the team checking the road out of town should spot him. Meanwhile, we've got to get on with the search."

"I know." She slid out, grabbing her own flashlight and zipping her jacket against the cold. "I wasn't trying to second-guess you."

He nodded. "Second-guess away, if you want. I know you care about him."

"Yes." *And about you.* But that was something she'd probably never have a chance to say.

Mitch swept his light in a wide circle, illuminating shrubs, trees, barren flower beds. "Let's start with the front. Check under every hedge."

She nodded and followed him into the yard, whispering a silent prayer.

They worked their way through one yard, then a second. Mitch was an organized, meticulous searcher, leaving nothing to chance. For the most part they worked in silence, occasionally consulting in low voices.

Three houses later she paused after checking under a lilac bush and watched Mitch swing a beam of light through low-hanging branches. "You act as if you've done this a lot. Conducted a search, I mean."

He bent to direct his light under a porch. "Often enough. We have a pretty well-organized search-and-rescue routine. It's a lot more difficult when someone's lost in the woods."

He straightened, looking up, and she followed the direction of his gaze. The bulk of the mountain was black against a paler black sky, looming over the town in an almost menacing way.

She shivered a little. Maybe people who lived here all the time got used to the mountain's presence. She hadn't, yet. Often it seemed protective, but tonight she was aware of its dangers.

"Davey wouldn't go up there. Would he?"

The beam of the flashlight showed her the tight line of his mouth. "I don't think so. I hope not."

"Please, Father." The prayer came out almost involuntarily. "Please be with that child."

"You sound like Simon Richie. I'm sure he's praying and searching at the same time."

The strained note in his voice caught her by surprise. "Aren't you?"

He shrugged. "I guess I figure God wants me to get on with my job, not go running to Him every time things get tough."

She checked a row of trash cans. Nothing. "Don't you think the Father wants to hear from His children when they're in trouble?"

Mitch swung his light toward her, maybe in surprise. For a moment he didn't say anything. Then, his voice harsh, he said, "I don't know. I don't have much experience with a good father."

The undertone of bitterness in his voice startled her. She kept forgetting, God forgive her. She kept forgetting how complicated his feelings were toward his own father. If that had spilled over into his relationship with his Heavenly Father, it wasn't surprising.

Be careful, she warned herself. *Don't make things worse.*

"I know what you mean." She tried to keep it

light. "If I believed God was a father like mine, I'd never be able to pray at all."

He stopped, the flashlight motionless in his hand. Had she gone too far?

Then he nodded. "Maybe you've got something there." His hand closed over hers warmly. "Let's search and pray."

An hour later they'd completed their grid as best they could. Looked like he'd been wrong about where the kid was likely to be found, Mitch thought. Where *was* he?

He slid into the cruiser next to Anne. She was shivering a little, and he started the heater before flipping the radio switch.

"Wanda. Got anything?"

"Nothing, Chief, sorry. Most teams have finished their first grid and gone on to their second." Wanda sounded briskly efficient. "You have anything?"

"Nada." His jaw clenched. Where was the kid? "I'll check in again in an hour."

Anne stirred beside him, leaning forward to look down the empty street. "Every house has its porch light on."

He nodded. "Word's spread. People want Davey to know he could walk up to any door in town right now."

"I didn't—" Anne's voice sounded choked. "I hope he sees. And understands."

"Yeah. Me, too."

Davey, where are you? Where did you run to?

Where would he run? Mitch tried to look at it rationally. If he were the kid, where might he go?

Home? But Davey didn't have a home, not anymore. Flagler had never bothered to provide his son with even minimum security.

Some people thought they didn't have homeless people in Bedford Creek. He knew better. Maybe they didn't have people sleeping on the streets, but there were those who didn't have a safe place to live.

Home. The word kept coming to him, refusing to go away. *Home.*

Are you trying to tell me something, Lord?

He glanced at Anne. That was the kind of conversation she probably had with God all the time. He hadn't realized, until tonight, that it was lacking in his own life. Or why.

He started the engine, and Anne looked at him.

"Where do we go next?"

He shrugged. "Maybe I'm wrong, but I've got a feeling. Let's go down to River Street and have a look at the place where Davey used to live."

A few minutes later they pulled up in front of a dilapidated house. It was dark and appeared empty. Still, something inside Mitch kept driving him. He had to check it out.

He approached the front door and tried it, sensing Anne coming up behind him and looking over his shoulder. A brand-new padlock glinted in the light from his flash. Looked like the landlord hadn't been taking any chances. But there might be another way in, a way a kid would know.

"I'll check the back. Why don't you stay here?"

She nodded, rubbing her arms against the chill, and he stepped off the creaky porch.

He prowled around the house, checking windows. The side door, too, bore a shiny new padlock. No sign anyone could have gotten in, not even a skinny kid.

He stopped at the back of the house, shining his light along the black windows. Nothing. This had turned into been a wild-goose chase. He'd better get back to his assigned grid and stop following hunches. One of the other searchers would cruise this neighborhood, anyway.

As he turned, his light flickered across the dirt-bare space stretching between the house and the river. He stopped. The light touched a decrepit building sagging into itself at the edge of the river.

Check it. The voice in his mind was insistent. *Check it.*

He stalked toward the building—little more than a shed, really. There were plenty of other places that would be warmer and drier for a kid out in the night.

Still, something drove Mitch. He had to look. He grabbed the sagging door. It stuck tight, and for a moment he thought it was locked.

He rattled it, putting his shoulder into it. The door popped open.

He took a step forward, flashing the beam of light around the interior. Nothing. Some battered boxes, a stack of lumber on one side, broken glass littering the floor.

"Davey!" His voice echoed in the cold darkness. Futile. The kid wasn't here.

He turned away, stepping through the open doorway. Then just as he started to shut the door, something creaked behind him. He froze.

His hand tightened on the door frame, and he swung the light toward the lumber pile. There might be—could be—just enough room behind it for one small body.

"Davey?" He reached the stack, moved to the side of it and peered along the wall. "Davey? You there?"

"Go away!" The boy's voice was shrill. "Go away! I hate you!"

Chapter Fourteen

"Davey, listen to me."

Behind him, Mitch could hear Anne's running feet. She must have heard. He held out a warning hand. No use spooking the boy by having too many people around. From the corner of his eye he saw her stop.

"No!" A scrabbling noise accented Davey's answer. The kid was trying to get around him to the door.

"Come on, Davey, I just want to talk."

This time Davey didn't bother with a verbal answer. He just spurted past.

Mitch grabbed, caught the sleeve of a windbreaker, and pulled the boy toward him. He wrapped both arms around the kid, trying to still his frantic struggles.

"Let me go! I don't wanna be with you. Let me go!"

"Davey—" Mitch clamped his arms tighter "—you have to let me talk to you. To tell you I'm sorry."

The slightest pause in the boy's flailing encouraged him to continue. "Listen, I was wrong. I was mad about something else, and I snapped at you instead." *Just like my father used to do.* The lump in his throat threatened to choke him. "I was wrong."

"Yeah, you were." Davey sounded angry, but he stopped struggling. "That stupid history—"

"Hey, I wasn't wrong about that. You still have to do your homework." He eased the pressure of his grip. He could sense Anne moving closer, but kept his focus on Davey. "That's part of the bargain. But I should have helped you, not yelled at you."

"Yeah." The boy's voice was muffled. "I thought maybe you…"

He put his hand gently on the kid's head. "What did you think?"

"I figured you were going to tell me to get out." The words came out defiantly, but Mitch could hear the fear underneath. "So I just figured I'd go before you got around to it."

Pain was an icy hand around his heart. *Lord, give me the right words. Please.* It was the kind of prayer he'd never felt comfortable with, but it came out so naturally now, warming him.

"Hey, we have a deal, remember? I don't go back on a deal." He held the boy a little away from him, so he could see his face in the dim light. "You're going to stay with me until your dad comes back. Right?"

Davey nodded, then looked down at his toes. "What if I do something you don't like?"

"Then I might yell. But I wouldn't tell you to go. No way." That was what he'd always wanted, but never had—the assurance that someone was there, whatever he did, no matter what. Just always there. "You've got my word on it."

Holding his breath, he released the boy. "We okay now?"

Davey peered up at him. Apparently whatever he saw satisfied him. He nodded.

Some of the tension slipped away. "All right. Let's get you home."

"Okay."

Davey took a step away. Then he stopped, waiting while Mitch shut the rickety door. He fell into step beside him as they walked to the patrol car.

Anne's gaze met Mitch's as she joined them. Her eyes were bright with tears. She touched Davey lightly on the shoulder. "Hi, Davey. I'm glad you're okay."

Davey nodded. Then he slid into the cruiser. Anne brushed a tear away with the back of her hand and followed him.

Thank you, Lord. He got in and picked up the

mike to let Wanda know to end the search. *Thank you.*

Davey fidgeted.

"Mitch?"

"Yeah?" He glanced at the boy.

"People were looking for me?"

"You bet people were looking for you. What'd you think, we'd just let you go?" Mitch gestured down the street, where every porch light was on. "See those lights? They're for you. Because people heard you were out there and wanted you to know it was okay to come to them."

He could see the muscles in Davey's throat work. "You sure?" The kid's voice wavered.

"I'm sure."

With a little sigh, Davey leaned back against the seat, hands relaxing.

Mitch saw Anne surreptitiously wipe away another tear.

Davey would still be a handful; he was sure of that. But if this night had convinced the kid that people cared what happened to him, they'd come a long way.

Anne climbed a little stiffly from the car when they pulled up in front of Mitch's. They'd stopped at the burger hut for sandwiches, and Davey had wolfed down two. Now he looked so tired he could hardly hold his eyes open, and she was in about the same shape.

"I'll say good night now."

Mitch caught her arm. "Come in for a minute." His smile flickered.

She wanted to stay. She wanted to go. Finally she nodded.

As soon as they got inside and he'd disappeared up the stairs with Davey, she had second thoughts. What was the point of this? They'd said everything there was to say that afternoon, and still Mitch had shut her out. He had been ashamed or embarrassed about kissing her. Could she believe any of that had changed, just because they'd come together over Davey's crisis?

She picked up her jacket, then tossed it over the back of the chair. She wouldn't be a coward about this. If Mitch wanted to talk, they'd talk.

She was sitting in the living room, leafing through a copy of a police magazine, when he came back downstairs. He'd shed his jacket, and the sleeves of his flannel shirt were rolled back, as if he'd been helping Davey get washed up. He glanced at the magazine in her hands.

"Getting up to date on the latest weapon regs?"

She shook her head, let the magazine drop onto the end table. "How is he?"

"Okay." Mitch sank to the couch next to her and leaned back, closing his eyes. The lines of strain were obvious on his face. It had been a difficult night for all of them—Mitch, Davey, the searchers who'd looked and prayed.

"Thank heaven you thought of looking there."

Mitch sat up. "Thank heaven is right. Something led us straight to him."

Yes. Something… Someone…had. "A lot of people were praying."

"I know." His face relaxed a little. "Thanks for your help tonight. That's what I wanted to say." His hand closed over hers. "Thank you. For everything."

"You're welcome. You and Davey both."

"I don't want to let him down."

Was that what was eating at him? Doubts over his ability to care for Davey? "You won't."

He shrugged. "Donovans don't have a very good record." His tone was light, but she knew him well enough to hear the pain under the words. "My dad left. My mother escaped into a bottle. Link turns tail at the sight of responsibility."

Her heart hurt for him. He was so sure, so in control on the outside. But inside he measured himself by his family. That was obviously behind his determination not to have a family of his own. The fear he'd turn out just like his own father.

"Maybe…" She went slowly, trying to find the right words. "Maybe you inherited everyone's share of responsibility. Assist, protect, defend. Like that crest in your office."

His smile flickered. "Military Police. I adopted that motto when I went in. They're good rules. They let you know what's expected of you."

She could see so clearly the boy he must have been, trying to make up for a bad start by finding something solid to hang on to. "We all need that."

"I need something else, too." His eyes darkened. "I need to say how sorry I am. About today."

The quarrel seemed to have taken place an eternity ago. "It's all right."

"No, it's not." He smiled wryly. "You got to see the worst aspect of having a brother. He knows me better than anyone, so he can push all my buttons. I was wrong to let that come between us."

His fingers moved softly against her wrist, tracing circles on the delicate skin. Each touch seemed to go right to her heart.

"Yes." Her breath caught on the word. "You were wrong."

His dark brown gaze was intent on her face. "Will you let me make up for it?"

Some faint warning voice told her she was getting in too deep, in danger of being swept away, like that story he'd told her.

She could retreat to safer ground. Go back to being the person who'd decided against having a man in her life. It would be safer, but it wouldn't be better.

She touched his cheek, feeling warm skin, the faint prickle of beard. He put his hand over hers, pressing her palm against his skin.

Her heart was so full that it stole the words. But she knew she loved him. She'd seen it coming, tried to avoid it, but nothing had done any good. She loved him.

Mitch drew her into his arms. She could feel the steady beat of his heart as she wrapped her arms around him. Her own heart threatened to overflow. She held him tightly. They had both come home at last.

Mitch lingered at the kitchen table over a second cup of coffee the next morning. Davey had gone off to school a little heavy-eyed, grumbling a bit, but he'd gone. At least he'd seemed confident Mitch would be there when he came home.

He lifted the cup to his lips, smiling. Funny thing, how he'd found himself smiling at odd moments ever since last night. Ever since he'd held Anne in his arms and dared to think about having a family.

Given the way Anne felt about Emilie, given the family wars she'd been through herself, she wouldn't trust a new relationship easily. But she'd taken the first painful steps from behind her safety barricades, and so had he.

Noise in the hallway wiped the smile from his face. It was stupid of him to tense at the very sound of his brother's footsteps.

If just knowing Anne could bring him this far from the person he'd been, he ought to be able to get through one breakfast conversation with his brother without snapping. He could try, anyway.

Link wandered through the doorway, spotted the

coffeepot and made straight for it. He didn't glance at Mitch until he'd taken several long gulps from his mug.

Maybe it was up to Mitch to get the conversational ball rolling. "How did your reunion go?" At least he hadn't heard any damage reports, so it couldn't have been too wild a time.

An expression of disgust crossed Link's face. "You wouldn't believe it. The old gang is going domestic. Getting married, buying houses, having kids...I thought I was in an old television rerun."

Mitch grinned. "Wedding bells are breaking up the old gang, huh?"

"That might be okay for them." Link responded with an answering grin that reminded Mitch of the little brother who'd once looked up to him. "But it's definitely not in my plans."

"What are your plans?"

Link shrugged. "The company wanted to send me to Anchorage on a project, but I turned it down." He shook his head. "Not for me. A two-year commitment, responsibility of crew chief...definitely not for me."

That was Link all over: running from any hint of something settled. "A little responsibility isn't a bad thing," Mitch said. He tried to keep the words light, but he could tell from the tightening of Link's expression that he didn't succeed.

"This town is getting to you, big brother. Be responsible, settle down, act just like everybody else and maybe they'll like you. Maybe they'll forget what you came from.''

His hand tightened on the coffee cup. ''That's not what's important to me.''

''Sure it is.'' Link slammed his mug down on the table. ''You think I don't know? I watched you at that fall festival when the mayor called you up on stage, said what a great job you'd done. You were eating it up. You'd have licked his boots for that praise.''

Link's words moved slowly through his mind. The foliage festival Link meant wasn't the most recent one. It was the one before.

His heart turned to lead. It was the one that was held when Tina Mallory was in town, when Link wasn't supposed to have been anywhere near Bedford Creek.

He looked at his brother. ''That was the festival before last. I thought you weren't here then.''

He could see the wheels turning in Link's mind, see him backpedaling. See him deciding it didn't matter.

''Yeah, so? That was after you'd told me never to darken your door again. I didn't bother to tell you I was in town. Place was so crowded with tourists, you'd never have noticed unless I'd walked right up to you. I wanted to see my buddies.''

''And who else did you see?'' The words tasted like ashes in his mouth.

''What do you mean?''

"I mean Tina Mallory." He could see it, rolling inexorably toward him. Link and Tina Mallory. Emilie. He almost didn't need to ask. He knew the truth, bone deep, and it was crushing him.

"Tina?" Link shrugged, turning away, not meeting his eyes. "Don't know her."

"You did." Mitch stood, feeling as if he forced his way upward against a huge weight. He pressed his fists against the table. "You knew her. You went out with her. You left her pregnant."

"Pregnant?" Link's face lost its color. "What are you talking about?"

"Tina Mallory. Cute little kid who worked at the café. A little kid you got pregnant." He hammered the words at his brother. "She's dead now, if you care."

"No!"

He could see Link's mind working feverishly, trying to find an excuse, an evasion. He felt suddenly very tired, as if the past had rolled over him and flattened him, and he'd never be right again.

"Don't bother to deny it. I can see the truth in your face."

A hunted look flickered in Link's eyes. "All right, I dated her a couple times. We got close. But I didn't know anything about a baby. I went back to the job. Tried to call her maybe a couple months later, but she'd left town. I never heard from her again. She never told me anything about any baby."

Given Link's history, the words rang true, but it

didn't seem to make much difference whether his brother had known about the baby or not. He could only think it was the end of everything.

"It wasn't my fault!" Link slammed his fist down on the table. "I know what you're thinking, but it wasn't just me. It was her, too."

"She was a kid."

"She was old enough to know what she was doing. And if you think you're going to tangle me up in this, you're wrong." He thrust away from the table and reached the back door almost before he finished speaking.

"Wait a minute." Mitch reached toward him. "We have to talk about this. For once in your life you have to face your responsibility."

"*You* talk about it, big brother. I'm getting out of here." He flung open the door before Mitch could get around the table, then looked back over his shoulder. "And think about this, while you're at it. The only reason she even went out with me was because I was your brother."

That stopped Mitch in his tracks. "What are you talking about?"

"That's right." The old mocking, defiant Link was back. "She went out with me because she had a crush on you, and you never gave her the time of day."

He slammed out.

Mitch stared at the door, pain wrapping around his heart. It looked as if he and Link, between them, had just proved that everything people had ever said about the Donovans was true.

That was what Anne would think. *Anne.* A fresh spasm of pain hit him.

He had to tell her, even though it might mean the end of everything between them.

There was only one thing he could do before he faced Anne with the truth. He'd catch up with Link and make him agree to sign the papers before he disappeared again. At least he could spare Anne that much pain.

She'd take the baby... *His niece.* An even stronger pain slammed his heart, shattering it. She'd take Emilie and the papers, and leave. He'd never see them again.

He wasn't sure how he'd go about living with that.

Chapter Fifteen

❧

"There we go, sweetheart." Anne snapped Emilie's romper. "All clean and dry and happy."

Emilie waved both arms, seeming ready to launch herself into space from her diaper change. Anne lifted her, planting a kiss on the soft round cheek.

"That's my girl. We'll just go downstairs and maybe..."

Maybe they'd look out the window and see Mitch? That was what she was thinking; she couldn't deny it.

Happiness seemed to bubble up inside her. Last night had been frightening, but it had been good, too. Thanks to Davey, she and Mitch had found their way past some of the barriers between them.

Arms snug around Emilie, she started down the steps. For the last eight months, she'd believed having Emilie in her life was all she'd ever need to be happy. Now…now she was looking beyond just herself and Emilie, to the possibility of a real family.

Even a month ago she wouldn't have thought it possible. But she'd already trusted Mitch more than she'd ever trusted anyone in her life. Maybe she really could take that next step, a step toward the kind of emotional intimacy she'd never imagined having. If she and Mitch could reach that, they'd share the kind of love she'd never believed would be hers.

The telephone rang in the hall below, and Kate rushed in from the kitchen to snatch it up, smiling at Anne and Emilie as they came down the stairs.

"Good afternoon. The Willows."

She listened for a moment, then held the receiver out to Anne.

"It's for you. Let me take that sweet child while you're talking."

Anne exchanged Emilie for the telephone. Kate, cooing to the baby, walked back toward the kitchen.

Anne lifted the receiver. Mitch? There was no reason to think he'd call this afternoon, but even so her heart beat a little faster. "Hello?"

"This is Marcy Brown." The girl's voice was hesitant. "You wrote me about Tina?"

Her stomach turned over, and she gripped the receiver. Marcy Brown, at last. "I'm so glad you called. And sorry I had to break such bad news to you. The thing is, Marcy, I need to find the baby's birth father in order to finalize the adoption. I'm hoping you can tell me something about him.''

Silence seemed to press along the connection.

''I—I don't...well, didn't Tina tell you who it was?''

Careful, careful. ''Tina mentioned one name. Mitch Donovan. But I know he's not the father, and I can't begin to guess why Tina would lie about it.''

Marcy's sigh came over the line clearly. ''She said that, did she? I told her not to, but she wouldn't listen.''

''You know, then.'' The blood seemed to be pounding in her ears. ''You know who Emilie's father is. You know why she named Mitch.''

''Yeah, well, that part's nuts, but Tina went off the deep end sometimes. Thing was, she really liked the chief, always talked about how nice he was to her and what a great guy he was. I think maybe when she realized the other guy was gone and wasn't coming back, she sort of pretended. You know, pretended that Mitch Donovan was the one, so everything would be all right. She didn't mean any harm by it... At any rate, it was Link Donovan. You know who I mean? The chief's brother.''

The hallway did a slow spin around her, and she sank down abruptly on the bench. ''How... But how can that be? I thought he wasn't even in Bedford Creek when Tina was here.'' That was what Mitch had said. He wouldn't lie to her.

''He was there—''

Anne could almost hear the shrug.

"—just for a couple weeks in the fall. It seems to me I did hear him say he didn't want his brother to know he was in town. Like they'd had some big fight or something."

The certainty settled on her like a weight. Mitch had mentioned the quarrel. Probably he'd never suspected Link was back in Bedford Creek at the crucial time.

"You're sure?"

"Oh, yeah. He was the only guy she went out with, and I think she just went with him because he sort of reminded her of the chief."

"I understand." She did. Tina, reaching out for love, had snatched at whatever was offered. But it hadn't been love.

A few more exchanges, a promise to send a photo of Emilie, and Anne put down the receiver. She knew now. She had the information she'd come to Bedford Creek to find.

And after asking Kate to watch Emilie, she headed out to find Mitch.

Ten minutes later, she stopped on the sidewalk outside the police station, stomach knotting. This would be difficult, so much more difficult than that first day, and she'd thought nothing could be worse than that.

Help me, Lord. Help me find the words. This news is going to hurt Mitch so much. I don't want to cause him pain, but he has to know.

She took a deep breath and opened the door.

Wanda looked up at her entrance, smiled, and waved her toward the inner office door.

Anne tapped, then opened the door. Mitch stood at the desk, head bent, just hanging up the phone. Her heart gave a little jump at the sight of him. For an instant thoughts of her reason for being there slipped away, and she was back in his arms again the night before, knowing she loved him.

No. She couldn't let herself think about that, not now. Not when she had to tell him something that would hurt him so badly.

"Anne."

She half expected him to round the desk toward her, but he didn't. "I have some news," she said, then stopped. This was so difficult, but she had to do it. She'd tried handling everything on her own, and it hadn't worked. Surely she and Mitch had come far enough to deal with this together.

"What is it?" He did come around the desk then, reaching toward her as if expecting the worst.

"Marcy Brown called." There wasn't any way to say this but to get it out. "She knew about Tina's pregnancy. Knew who the father was." She swallowed hard. "She even knew why Tina named you."

He didn't say anything, just stared at her from under lowered brows, his face expressionless. The mask was back in full force, as if he needed its protection.

"She said…" She took a steadying breath. "She said it was Link."

There, it was out. Mitch would be shocked, denying it, but…

But he wasn't. He just stood there, looking at her, and she read the knowledge in his face.

"You already knew." The words were out before she thought about them. He *knew*.

Pain gripped her. All this time she'd been desperate to find the truth, all this time…

"How could you do this?" The blood pounded in her head. Later she'd need to weep, but not now. Now she had to react to this betrayal.

"Anne, it's not what you think."

"You knew how important this is. How could you lie to me?" Maybe she wouldn't be able to hold back the tears until later. They stung her eyes, salty and bitter.

"I didn't!"

Her heart turned to stone. "You knew. You didn't tell me. What is that but a lie?"

He reached out to her, as if to touch her, and she recoiled. He let his hand drop, eyes darkening.

"I didn't know, not until today. You can't believe I've been lying to you all along—"

"When today?" It was like being back in a courtroom, but she'd never tried a case that held so much personal anguish for her.

He stiffened. "This morning. Link told me the truth this morning."

"And you kept it from me." Her head throbbed. "How long were you going to keep it from me, Mitch? Until after he was gone again? Until he wasn't here in Bedford Creek to embarrass you?"

"No! That's not why I didn't tell you. Anne, you have to believe me. I only wanted—"

She shook her head. "You're wrong. I don't have to believe you." She could barely breathe against the heartache. "I was wrong ever to trust you. It's a mistake I won't make again."

Mitch stared at the door that had closed behind Anne—that closed on any chance he might have to make things right.

He could go after her, but what would he say? *I was wrong?* She knew that already, and nothing he could say would make it any different.

He'd ruined everything with his black stubbornness. If he'd gone to her with the truth right away, maybe there would have been some small chance to make things right. Now there was none.

He'd told himself he was trying to spare her, to delay telling her until he could find Link and try to repair the damage. But maybe she was right. Maybe he was really trying to spare himself.

He hadn't fixed anything. He'd lost his brother and he'd lost Anne, and this was one thing he couldn't blame on his father. This one was all his fault.

One way or another, he had to find Link. Getting

Link to cooperate wouldn't change things between himself and Anne. How could it? But at least it would make things right for her and Emilie. That was all he could expect.

Getting Link's signature was the only thing left Mitch could do for Anne, and he wasn't going to fail.

But two hours later the possibility of failure loomed a lot larger. He drove down River Street one more time. He'd tried every friend of Link's he could remember, tried every place his brother might be staying. He met nothing but blank looks. No one had seen his brother since the day before.

He seemed to be out of options. His stomach twisted. He'd have to see Anne, let her know what he was trying to do. She wouldn't want to see him, but he had to tell her he wouldn't give up until he had Link ready to sign.

He stopped in front of Kate's place, took the steps two at a time. He rapped on the door.

Kate swung it open and looked at him, her gaze a little startled. "Mitch. Is something wrong?"

"I need to see Anne. Will you let her know I'm here?"

But Kate was shaking her head. "I can't do that."

"What do you mean?" He could sense bad news coming, see it in the way her gaze slid away from his.

"Anne's gone." Kate gave a helpless little gesture. "I couldn't talk her out of it. She took the baby and went back to Philadelphia."

The road snaked ahead of Anne, glistening a little in the gray afternoon light. The cold, light rain slicked the pavement, and she slowed as she started up the steep hill. Maybe if she kept her mind on the road conditions, she could keep the pain at bay a little longer.

It didn't seem to be working. Her breath caught on a little sob.

Mitch, how could you do this? How could you betray me this way?

Emilie wiggled in her car seat, just beginning to fuss. She hadn't been happy to be packed up so abruptly. And Kate…Kate hadn't understood at all, but Anne hadn't been able to explain her sudden need to leave.

She still couldn't, not even to herself. She'd just known she had to get away from Bedford Creek, away from Mitch.

"Hush, Emilie. It'll be all right. We'll be home soon."

That was what she needed to hear someone say to her. *It will be all right.* But there was no one to do that.

Why, Lord? she prayed bleakly. *Why did You let me begin to trust, begin to care, only to face betrayal?*

She could have handled the fact that Link was

Emilie's father. She could even understand Tina's convoluted reasoning in naming Mitch as the father.

Tina had thought Mitch was everything Link wasn't—solid, responsible, trustworthy. She'd probably thought she could count on Mitch to do the right thing.

Anger pulsed through her; she tightened her grip on the wheel. She'd thought that, too. And they'd both been wrong. He'd chosen to protect his brother instead of her and Emilie.

What would Link do? Her throat tightened. She should have stayed, tried to see him, tried to get his signature on the forms. That was why she'd come to Bedford Creek in the first place.

But she wasn't the person she'd been then. That Anne Morden would have put on her lawyer's armor and faced down both the Donovan brothers. Now she'd started to care too much, and she couldn't do it, not without letting Mitch see exactly how much he'd hurt her.

So she'd go home. She'd go back to Philadelphia, hire a private investigator, put the whole thing in professional hands.

Emilie's cry went up an octave, and Anne winced. She turned her head to take a look, and felt the car swerve. Her fingers tightened on the wheel. She must be more tired than she'd thought. She couldn't—

The car swerved again, sliding across the road, and she fought the steering wheel. It wasn't her—it was the rain. She touched the brake, barely tapping it. If she could just get onto the gravel berm, they'd be all right.

The car swung across the road, out of control. Her stomach turned over. She clenched the wheel, jerking it, but it was no good—she'd lost control entirely. They careened sideways, nothing between them and the steep drop-off but a narrow gravel stretch and a ditch.

She couldn't stop. Her mind flashed ahead to an image of her car sliding off the mountain, tumbling down the steep slope, plunging into the trees below.

Help us, Father! Help us!

Seconds became an eternity…spinning trees, whirling lights, frantic prayers. And then the car slid gently to rest against the opposite bank.

The sobs she heard were hers. Emilie's crying had stopped, maybe out of her amazement at the ride. Anne twisted in the seat, touching the baby with frantic hands.

"Are you all right? Emilie, are you okay?"

Emilie batted at her hands, then stretched, twisting irritably in the car seat.

She was all right. Anne leaned her forehead against the seat back. The baby was all right. They were both all right, no thanks to her.

"Thank you, Lord." She patted Emilie, then wiped away the hot tears that spilled down her cheeks. "Thank you."

I wasn't in control. But You were.

She turned, leaning back in the seat, relief flooding her. God had been in control. Even though she hadn't trusted, even though she'd been trying to do it all herself, God had been in control.

"I haven't been trusting You, have I?"

Helen would probably smile at the question. Wise Helen had seen what Anne needed. Believing wasn't enough. She had to trust, too.

She brushed her hair back from her forehead. "I'll try, Lord. I'll try."

She couldn't have a relationship with God unless she could trust. She couldn't have a relationship with another person unless she could trust.

She looked back over the last twenty-four hours. She'd told herself she loved Mitch, but she hadn't trusted him enough to give him a chance to explain. Maybe things could never be right between them; maybe there were too many barriers. But whatever happened, she couldn't run away. She had to give him a chance.

Something else was crystal clear in her mind. Unless Mitch could open up, unless he could find a way to deal with the family problems that haunted him, they didn't stand a chance.

Her heart turned to lead. Dealing with that pain might be more than Mitch was able to do. But she'd learned something in these difficult weeks. Having a relationship built on trust, based on openness, really was possible.

She'd never believed that before, but now she knew it. And she couldn't settle for less.

Slowly, carefully, she put the car in gear and started back toward Bedford Creek.

Chapter Sixteen

❧

"Look, just stay by the phone for me, okay?" Mitch frowned at Wanda. "I've asked half the town to call me if they spot Link. Someone's bound to see him."

"All right, all right." Wanda dropped the purse she'd picked up, preparing to going home. "But you owe me for this one."

He owed a lot of people—Anne most of all. But she was gone. He looked bleakly down the years he would be missing her. Why couldn't she have given him a few minutes' grace? That was all he'd wanted. Now—

He heard the door, spun around, and his breath caught in his throat. Anne stood there, holding the baby. He'd never seen a sweeter sight in his life.

She was pale, and she clutched Emilie too tightly. The baby wiggled restlessly.

"What's wrong?" He took a step toward her, battling pain, grief, regret. Something was wrong besides the obvious, but whatever it was, she probably wouldn't accept help from him. The only thing he had left to offer her was Link's signature on that form.

She shook her head. "Nothing. We're all right. We just… I decided we needed to come back."

"I'm glad you did." Easy, don't push. "I'm trying to find Link, so I can—"

The telephone rang, and he nearly leaped across the desk. Wanda said a few words, then hung up and turned to him. He could read the message on her face. Someone had spotted Link.

"Behind Grace Church. His truck's parked there."

Adrenaline pumped through his veins. Something positive to do, thank heaven. He turned to Anne.

"You wait here with Wanda. I'll find Link and bring him back."

But she was already shaking her head. "We'll go with you."

The last thing he wanted was Anne observing an ugly scene. "That's not a good idea. I'll do better with him alone."

"I'm going." Her mouth set stubbornly, she turned toward the door.

"Anne…"

Frustrated, he shook his head. He didn't want her

there when he confronted his brother. But it didn't look as if he had a choice.

If he'd picked the worst place in the world to confront his brother, this would be it, Mitch thought as he pulled up to Grace Church Cemetery. His throat tightened. Link was on one knee in front of a double headstone, carefully clearing away the dried leaves that littered it. He looked very young, kneeling there in the brown grass in front of their parents' graves.

Mitch and Anne's footsteps grated on a patch of gravel. Link swung around, his face hardening when he saw them. "What are you doing here?"

"Looking for you." Mitch stared down at his parents' headstone. "Guess I should have thought sooner to look here."

"Why would you?" Link stood, fists clenching. "Not a place you spend much time, is it?"

"I guess not." He stared down at the epitaph. At his father's name. His father hadn't come back until it was too late to say the things that needed to be said between them. Maybe he could keep from making the same mistake with Link. "Look, we need to talk."

Link shrugged, his face cold. "I've got nothing to say."

"Fine, just listen, then." He couldn't let himself think about Anne, standing so silently beside him.

"Sorry, don't have time." Link spun, but Mitch grabbed his arm.

"Make time, Link. This is important."

"To you?" His expression made it clear that didn't weigh with him.

"To this baby girl." He jerked his head toward Emilie, his eyes never leaving Link's face. "She deserves a chance in life."

Link's gaze swiveled to Anne and the pink snow-suited bundle she carried. "Tina's baby." Link said it with certainty.

"That's right. How did you know?"

He shrugged. "Wasn't hard to figure out, once I knew part of it. Why else would Anne and the baby be in Bedford Creek?"

"Listen to me, Link." His throat was so tight that he had to force the words out. "When Tina knew she wasn't going to make it, she wanted Anne to adopt her baby. She wanted to give her a chance at a good future."

"Okay, I'm giving her that chance, too." Link's gaze slid away from the baby. "I'm getting out of here. That's the best thing I can do for her." He nodded toward the headstone. "After all, that's what he did for us. Like father, like son, right? He just should have done it sooner."

The bitterness in his brother's voice seeped into Mitch's heart. He was used to it in himself. He'd never guessed it ran so deeply in Link. He felt a sudden revulsion. It wasn't doing either one of them any good.

"Don't, Link. Don't think that about yourself."

"Why not? It's true, isn't it?"

Conviction pounded through his veins. He knew, now, what he had to do. What they both had to do, if only it wasn't too late.

"What he did doesn't matter anymore. At least, it only matters if we let it." He reached toward his brother. "Don't you see what we're doing? We're still letting him control our lives."

"Not you. Not Mr. Upright Citizen. Your life is as different as it can be from his."

"Don't you get it?" Mitch caught his brother's arm. He had to make him see. "I'm doing everything I can to be different from him. You're doing everything you can to be like him. That means we're both still letting him run our lives."

For a moment Link stared at him, dark eyes unreadable. "Yeah, well, there's not much we can do about that, is there?"

"We can stop." The conviction settled into his soul, so strong he didn't even mind the fact that Anne was hearing all of this. "We can forgive him."

He hadn't known it was true until he'd said it. A sense of release slid through him. All this time, trying to be the opposite of everything his father stood for, he'd still been holding on to his resentment. Letting it control his life.

Link jerked free of him. "I can't!" A shadow crossed his face. "And what difference would it make if I could? He's gone."

"It won't make a difference to him. Just to us."

He put his hand on Link's shoulder, feeling his brother tense at his touch. It drove a knife through his heart. He never should have let things get so bad between them. Link was the only family he had in the world, probably the only family he ever would have.

They stood side by side, looking down at their parents' graves. "Let it go, Link. Let them go."

"Not what you'd call a perfect set of parents, were they?" Bitterness still laced Link's words.

"No, I guess they weren't. But that doesn't mean we have to repeat their mistakes." His hand tightened on his brother's shoulder. "I haven't exactly been a perfect big brother, either. Maybe I can do better, if you give me a shot at it."

Mitch felt the tension begin to seep out of Link. "So…if I were trying to do better than they did…" He choked, but went on. "What would I do about this baby?"

That one Mitch knew the answer to. "Sign the papers so Anne can adopt." He looked at her, seeing the way she cradled the baby close, as if defying anyone to take her away. "Nobody could possibly be a better parent to that little girl than she will be."

Link looked at Anne and the baby, not speaking. Then he let out a long breath. "Okay. Let's do it."

Mitch's eyes stung with unshed tears. He nodded. "Follow us back to the office. We can take care of it there."

A few minutes later Link stood by the desk in Mitch's office. His hands clenched into two tight fists. "I'm ready."

Anne looked shell-shocked, as if she couldn't handle much more. "Are you sure?"

Link took a step forward and touched Emilie's soft curls. An emotion—sadness?—crossed his face. Then he nodded.

"I'm sure. She belongs with the mother who loves her." His voice roughened. "I guess Tina knew that. I won't interfere."

Mitch tried to swallow the lump in his throat. This had been a long time coming, but he finally was getting to see his little brother step up and do the right thing, instead of running away. Maybe there was hope for Link…hope for both of them.

Anne juggled the baby as she fumbled with the catch to her bag.

"Let me take her." Mitch reached out, and Emilie came eagerly into his arms.

For a moment he thought Anne would snatch the baby back, but then she nodded.

Give me a chance, Anne. Give us a chance. He wanted to say it, but he couldn't.

Anne unfolded the paper slowly, then held it out to Link.

He took it to Mitch's desk, leaned over to read it.

A muscle worked in his jaw, the only outward sign of his feelings. He reached for a pen and scrawled his signature in a quick slash across the bottom of the page.

Anne's breath escaped in an audible sigh. She had to be thinking that it was over, that Emilie was safe at last.

Link handed the paper to her, and she folded it quickly.

"That's that, then." Link tried to smile, but it didn't quite work. "You don't need to worry I'll cause problems. I won't."

Mitch's heart hurt for Link. His little brother had finally started to grow up, but it was a painful process.

"What are you going to do?"

Link shrugged. "Think I'll take on that job in Alaska I told you about." He aimed a light punch at Mitch's arm. "Who knows? Next time I come back, I might have turned into a responsible citizen. Like my big brother."

"Stranger things have happened."

Link glanced from him to Anne. "Looks to me like you could stand to talk things out."

Mitch, cradling Emilie in his arms, nodded. *If Anne will talk to me, that is.*

Link crossed to the door, then looked at them. "You know, I'm not cut out to be a father." He paused. "But I think I could be a darn good uncle, if the position opens up."

He closed the door before either of them could respond.

Anne looked at her baby…hers now, for good. The three of them were alone here, just as they'd been that first day when she came to break the news to Mitch. Emilie was perfectly happy in Mitch's arms.

"We do need to talk." Mitch's voice was a low rumble.

She nodded. "I guess that's why I came back. I couldn't…"

How could she say it? The words didn't seem to exist to explain the tangled emotions she felt at the sight of him.

Mitch looked at Emilie's face, as if trying to discern some resemblance to his brother. "I really didn't think it could be Link. I was so sure he wasn't in town when Tina was here. Sure that was one thing I couldn't blame on him."

"I know." She hesitated, feeling her way. They had to get this out between them. "But I don't know why you didn't tell me when you found out."

Because you couldn't trust me? Just like I couldn't trust you?

He shook his head. "How can I make you understand? The truth just hit me like a sledgehammer. All I could think was that it proved the Donovans were just as bad as everyone always said."

She saw the anguish in his face as he said the words, and it reached out and gripped her heart, too.

"I wouldn't have thought that. I don't think it now. Link was wrong, but at least he's starting to face up to it."

"Maybe he'd have faced it sooner if I hadn't blown up at him." He touched Emilie's hand, and she latched onto his finger. "Anne, you have to know I never intended to hurt you and Emilie. I just wanted a chance to find Link and clear things up with him before I told you. That's all. I would have told you today." He looked at her, dark eyes intense. "I wish you could believe that."

Her heart started to pound. He wanted to know she trusted him. Was that so much to ask?

"You…you and Link have made a start at working things out." That wasn't what she wanted to say. Why was it so hard to tell him what she felt?

He nodded. "The truth is, I let my feelings about my father color everything else in my life. My relationship with my brother, my career, even my relationship with you. I finally saw I had to forgive him, if I wanted any kind of a future." He looked at her, his dark eyes steady. "What about you, Anne? Are you ready to put the past to rest so we can move on?"

That was the question she'd started to face out on that road. She'd let her relationship with her parents govern her relationship with God, just as Mitch had.

She hadn't even recognized she was doing it. It was time for both of them to stop.

She looked at Mitch holding her child, and her heart swelled. "I'd like to try."

The love in his eyes took her breath away. "We've got a few hurdles to get over. But God's not finished with us yet." He took a step toward her. "I love you, Anne. I want to try and make this work. Will you stay? Will you marry me?"

If she didn't take this chance, she knew she'd miss the best God had to offer her. She moved forward, letting Mitch's arms enfold both of them. "We'll stay."

Epilogue

"Da, da, da, da!" Emilie stood in the stroller and banged on the tray.

"All right, Sweetheart." Anne maneuvered the stroller through the summertime crowds on the sidewalk. "We'll go to the station and see Mitch."

The baby plopped back into her seat, apparently satisfied. Emilie hadn't mastered the sound of "Mitch" yet, but that didn't matter. After their wedding this fall, he really would be her daddy.

Anne dodged a tourist with a camera and pushed through the station door. Wanda gave her a welcoming smile.

"Chief!" she shouted. "Anne's here."

Davey dropped the broom he'd been wielding and rushed to Emilie. "Can I take her out of the stroller, please? I want to show Wanda how she can walk."

"Of course." Anne smiled. Emilie held her arms out to the person she considered a big brother, and he lifted her carefully from the stroller.

In the months Davey had been living with Mitch, he'd blossomed. That wary, sullen look was completely gone from his eyes. Neither his father nor any other relative had been located, but Davey's permanent placement with Mitch gave him the security he'd never had before. Perhaps, one day, she and Mitch would be able to adopt him legally, but that wouldn't make him any more their son than he already was.

Trust in the Lord with all your heart. She still had to remind herself of that each day. God would work out what was right for Davey, in His own time.

The office door opened, and Mitch came toward her quickly. "Anne." Love shone in his eyes as he kissed her. The mask he'd once worn was gone now entirely, and his face no longer hid his emotions. His feelings were written plainly for her to read.

His arm still around her, Mitch reached for Davey and Emilie. The baby toddled toward them, clutching Davey's hand, beaming.

Mitch swept Emilie up in his arms, and Anne put her hand on Davey's shoulder, drawing him close.

Family. They were a family. She looked up at Mitch, her heart overflowing with love. She hadn't really known the meaning of the word before. Now, each day, she and Mitch discovered how deep, how blessed their love could be.

She'd come to Bedford Creek to find Emilie's father. God had seen to it that she found so much more.

* * * * *

Be sure to watch for Brett Elliot's romance,

THE DOCTOR NEXT DOOR,

*coming to Love Inspired
in June 2000.*

Dear Reader,

What happens when a man is confronted with the claim that he fathered a child, a claim he knows isn't true? Mitch Donovan popped into my mind one day, complete with all the baggage of a difficult family background that had made him determined never to have children of his own. All I knew about the story was that he'd fall in love with a woman who came complete with baby, and that he wouldn't be able to have the love God intended for him until he learned to forgive.

Thank you for reading my book. I hope you enjoyed Mitch and Anne's story, and that you'll look forward to visiting Bedford Creek again.

I love to hear from readers, and I hope you'll write to me c/o Steeple Hill Books, 300 East 42nd Street, New York, NY 10017.

Best wishes,

Marta Perry